TALES OF PAST AND PRESENT

TALES OF PAST AND PRESENT

Henry Tedeschi

iUniverse, Inc.
New York Lincoln Shanghai

Tales of Past and Present

iUniverse books may be ordered through booksellers or by contacting:

iUniverse
2021 Pine Lake Road, Suite 100
Lincoln, NE 68512
www.iuniverse.com
1-800-Authors (1-800-288-4677)

This is a work of fiction. All of the characters, names, incidents, organizations, and dialogue in this novel are either the products of the author's imagination or are used fictitiously.

The credits for the cover should be: Painting: Sylvia Chessin, Graphics: Maria Sohn.

ISBN: 978-0-595-44573-8 (pbk)
ISBN: 978-0-595-88899-3 (ebk)

Printed in the United States of America

Contents

THE CHAMELEON

Vickie didn't know why she had married Edward Holmit. From the distance of three years, it seemed a very foolish thing to have done. They had nothing in common. Edward was so stiff, you'd think somebody had stuck a broom handle up his ass. When they had first met, he had seemed glamorous with his unconcern for what he spent on her. Now she felt, she had been just a possession he'd coveted, although to give him his due, he wasn't after collecting material things. Vickie didn't really know what he was after. He didn't voice an interest in books, literature, museums or art in general. In their first year they had tried for a baby. Eventually when it hadn't happened, she felt only relief and even started on the pill, even though she knew she was unlikely to conceive without it. She didn't know who was at fault. She assumed it was Ed—he was the one lacking emotion.

Vickie thought she might have agreed to marry him to leave behind her dysfunctional family, an emotional drain even if it was no longer a daily stress once she'd moved out. Still, she'd tired of arguments between her mother and stepfather and the bickering over her younger sister who Vickie found impossible to protect. Occasionally, they would even turn on her. They seemed to enjoy a squabble as if they were competing for points in a contest. I made an ass out of you: that's five points. I hurt your feelings: that's ten points. I showed that you are entirely wrong: that's another ten points.

Most of the time she had eventually been on her own. Vickie had had four trouble-free years when in college. After that, of course, she'd had her own apartment. The job at the museum provided her with just enough money to survive without discomfort. But it was a rather drab life. She still saw her girlfriends but after a while most of them had married. Vickie was tired of hearing about colic, diapers and staying up all night.

Then Edward had made his appearance. Relatively handsome, he earned a wonderful salary. At the time, she was not quite sure what he did for a living. He had a hand in investing and transferring funds. The company's name, Bolton International, didn't reveal much about its business activities.

Her previous boyfriends had not been interested in making a commitment aside from sharing her bed. There were moments of ecstasy and delight. But after a while the relationships became routine and seemed to have no future. After several dates, Edward actually went on his knees to propose just like in romantic novels of yesteryear.

She had to admit that their first year together was full of excitement. Buying the proper house in the suburbs. Redecorating, furnishing it with care. But then there followed two dismal years. Fortunately, Ed had found her a job at Bolton. Assistant to the CEO no less. George Rapidde, a dashing and glamorous man, had come from nowhere to become one of the most celebrated successes of the business world. Sometimes she felt her work was only that of a secretary—although not exactly as it was well paid and a step forward.

Her job made life more bearable, yet Vickie had become sufficiently concerned about her personal life to discuss it with Millie. Since college, she had been very close to Millie and at that time they had always exchanged confidences. Millie had eventually married and produced one baby after another. The two of them no longer had that much in common.

When listening to Vickie's complaints, Millie finally said, "I think you're ready for an affair."

Vickie laughed. "Is that what you have been doing?"

"What has that got to do with your problems? I have babies and toddlers coming out of my ears. I wouldn't have the time to even think about an affair!"

Vickie had assumed that the taunt was to tease her, but Millie's words reverberated in her mind.

Part of Vickie's job was to accompany George Rapidde when he was negotiating some deal out of town. She had come to appreciate those trips. The hotels where they stayed provided unexpected distractions and luxuries. George Rapidde, he had become George by then, was a pleasure to be with—always amusing and considerate. The negotiations usually were intense interactions lasting for a day or two. She took extensive notes but was more of a spectator than a participant, although George sometimes solicited her opinion and listened attentively. She felt comfortable being seen with such an attractive and powerful man. When finally they spent an evening dancing, the transition to bed seemed most natural. An experienced lover, he brought her suspense and thrills she had never suspected possible. His love making was a teasing, loving experience until the two bodies joined in the sex act.

She found her duplicity hard to maintain. Something in her mind kept telling her that she was being a double-crossing bitch, particularly since she had been unable to keep Ed away from her. Finally, one evening after a silent dinner, expecting a dreadful scene, she announced that she had something to tell him. She told him she had been involved with another man, although she didn't reveal his identity.

Vickie felt completely drained by the tension that preceded her revelation. Ed's response was unexpected. As if crushed by her disclosure, he sat silently for a few moments. Then Ed spoke as if his mouth had trouble forming words. To her surprise, Vickie felt sorry for him. He wasn't a bad man. His words came in short interrupted sentences.

"I can't say I'm completely surprised … I'm a hard man to live with … I'm sorry I failed you." Ed seemed unable to continue for a few moments. "If you want a divorce, that's up to you. If you want to try again with me, I'll do my best."

Vickie felt she had some insight into Ed. He had grown up without love from his parents and that had taken its toll. But knowing that wasn't much help. She didn't know how to deal with their situation after her revelation. They continued living together possibly because of her inertia, although they no longer slept in the same room. Yet she felt that the situation was very unfair to Ed. To complicate matters George's attentions seemed to have cooled. His love making had become routine and at every opportunity he criticized her work performance. It all seemed to have started when she had discovered a record of a transfer of funds for which she could not find a good reason.

She wasn't a person to avoid facing problems. In George's office she looked him right in the eye after he had taken issue with something she had done.

"What's going on George?"

"Don't tell me you haven't been reading the papers or watched television?"

"I have no idea what you're talking about."

"You may be asked to testify. I want you to leave town immediately and make yourself scarce. Go to Europe, Hawaii. Some place far away. We'll cover your expenses."

This man, who had been a cherished lover, now saw her only as a possible danger. Vickie had no idea of what had happened. With her situation with Ed still unresolved, she was not going to suddenly disappear.

"Just tell me what's going on."

"You already know too much. If you know what's good for you, you'll follow my directions."

"If you'd ever tried to understand where I'm coming from, you'd know that I don't follow commands, unless there is a good reason that I fully understand."

"You little bitch! Okay. Let's put it this way. I have enough stuff on you to force you." He was now angry. He pulled some photographs out of a drawer and dropped them in front of her. A sudden intake of breath expressed her shock. These were the most explicit pictures of raw sex she'd ever seen. If she hadn't known that those things had happened during her affair with George, she would have thought they were faked.

"You bastard. And I even thought you cared for me."

"We all have our favorite illusions. I can't say we didn't have fun, but now it's time for some serious business."

"You bastard!"

"If you don't want these posted on the web you'd better be reasonable."

"You bastard!"

"Well, I guess you need a little bit of softening to find out what it feels like."

He picked up the phone and pressed a button. "Please ask Mr. Holmit to come to my office."

Anguish filled her very being. Poor Ed was going to be tormented again and none of this was really his fault. "You bastard!" And she covered her face. She would have thought that it wouldn't hurt her now that she had almost separated from Ed, but she was wrong and she was terrified.

There was a sound of a door opening. "Come in! Come in!" Then silence.

She looked up dreading what she would see, either Ed in shock or looking at her with loathing on his face, but all she could see on his face was an uncontrollable fury. He had changed, the way a chameleon can change color when needed.

"You try to hurt my wife again and I'll kill you."

George's voice had changed despite the sneer in his voice. "Don't you dare threaten me. I've got enough on you so that you'll spend the rest of your life in jail."

"You're not listening. Dead is dead. Check my background. My grandfather was Corsican. That's the blood in my veins."

"Is that what he would have done if he'd found out that his wife was a strumpet?"

"Honor has many facets. Hurt my wife again and you'll find out."

George was now sneering, "A strumpet!"

Vickie had never considered Ed to be powerful and she knew that George spent much of his time working out, but it was George who ended up groaning on the floor holding his stomach. For the first time in her life Vickie appreciated the male propensity for violence.

"Let's go Vickie. We are not wanted here."

Ed picked up the photographs and held them in one hand. He extended his other hand and held hers as they exited the office.

Ed's fury abated as they entered their house.

"Did you really mean that you were going to kill him?"

"I certainly felt like it. I still do."

"Please! Don't even think of it. He isn't worth it. I'm really the villain of the piece. You can't imagine how I felt when he showed you the pictures. I thought I was going to die!"

Vickie felt like crying and laughing at the same time. She chose her mischievous side.

"Was your grandfather really Corsican?"

"Absolutely! My mother's dad. He was a cobbler. He came to this country to make a decent living and he wasn't capable of hurting a fly!" Ed was also laughing.

It occurred to her that they hadn't laughed together since their courtship. It felt good but didn't diminish her anxiety.

"What did he mean about putting you in jail for life?"

"Apparently a good deal of money has been diverted. Probably to George's accounts. As you know I did all the transferring. But I didn't make the decisions and had no idea what the transfers were for. But it will show on my computer. I hope it will become clear from the testimonies that I wasn't responsible."

"Oh, shit! Let's make sure."

"What are you going to do?"

"You forget I'm the CEO's personal assistant, I haven't been fired and I haven't quit. I can fiddle with the computers. I have all the passwords and details. I can transfer the information from your computer to his."

"Vickie! I don't want you to go back there. That man is insane. He might hurt you."

"Well come with me. You can stay in your office. We can keep in touch through our cellular phones. It won't take long."

And that was what they did.

For some time, these events remained in their minds as a bad dream. But later, Vickie and Ed became too busy with the babies. Millie was quite right. They are incredibly demanding, even with the two of them trying their best.

Watching their latest addition cradled in Ed's arms, Vickie wondered how she could have ever thought that he was incapable of loving.

JUNE

She was called June. He never found out whether that was her real name. There was never a long wait, unless it was Wednesday, payday in the steel mills. The evening trolley ride took half an hour to the gray frame houses in a row, their innards divided into small rooms by wooden partitions. There generally was a madam, directing the women and the men visitors. All the half-naked women in the front hall were various shades of black. A chum from college had taken him there, window shopping so to speak, going from house to house. The hard-bitten women were somber and unappetizing even to a boy of eighteen overwhelmed by hormones and desire.

Yet he found himself returning after a few weeks. That's when he saw June. She couldn't have been older than eighteen or nineteen. Light-skinned, her body followed classical lines. Not the Rubenesque figures of the paintings but along the lines of the Greek statues of antiquity. More importantly, she smiled at him—a sad smile, full of friendship, devoid of artifice.

What followed he could have expected. After he quickly undressed in her cubicle, after a careful examination, she washed his member with water at body temperature. Part of the intent, he imagined, was hygienic, part erotic. Then the unexpected happened. As he was holding her naked body overwhelmed by desire, she kissed him on the lips. More of a passionate kiss than a professional ploy. He felt overwhelmed. Kissing in a whorehouse, he had been told, was an emphatic no-no. Kissing a woman was also completely outside his experience. Working his way through college and the intensity of the science courses had limited his life experiences. There had been a few hurried kisses when accompanying a girl home after a chaste date, but this had been entirely different.

As one might expect from a professional, she was nimble and skillful. She allowed him to linger and in fact he was able to arrive to more than one climax.

A knocking on the door by the madam made it clear that they had gone past the allotted time. June laughed at that.

Several visits followed, much the same. One time June was not there. Before leaving, he took a good look at the other women, none very attractive. He got the distinct feeling the madam emphatically disapproved of his fickleness and he left after some hesitation.

He and June rarely exchanged many words. He was curious about her life. Aside from her profession she seemed so conventional. Her words, as rare as they were, were gentle and articulate. He knew the horrible price extracted by racism and he felt considerable warmth for her. Out of curiosity he asked her what she did with her free time. His words elicited an unexpected response.

"You can take me out on my day off. But please, no sex. It's my day off."

He was moved by her response, although he didn't follow her suggestion. Life was complicated enough the way it was. In the trolley, returning to his dormitory, he was full of regret. He knew he would never see her again. He hadn't realized she had meant so much to him.

AGE BEFORE BEAUTY

Adam Recoust's country store in Burgherton was a natural place to spend time. A coffee pot was always ready on the coal stove and some would bring their own booze, which Recoust tolerated as long as nobody got too boisterous. Several seats were arranged around the pot-bellied stove that burned in the fall and winter, or when not inside the store in nice days visitors and Recoust would sit on the porch. He enjoyed telling many improbable but amusing stories.

Recoust was mostly bald with a straggly short white beard, innumerable folds crisscrossing his face and brown age stains on a pale skin. Generally, he was dressed in worn-out dungarees and a faded blue denim shirt. A Stetson wouldn't have been out of place, but he wore one only when going out which was almost never. He never shortchanged anybody in the store he ran. Many years before he had arrived from nowhere. His age was frequently subject to good-natured disputations. Some claimed that he must be one hundred years old. If he heard them, he just smiled. Although his hands were twisted by arthritis and his back was somewhat bent, the estimate seemed unlikely since he was rather spry.

He claimed to have been a drummer boy in Sherman's march to the sea. He would tell how as a cowboy, he had worked in the Dakota Bad Lands and in Abilene, where he had killed more than one man in gun duels. He would exhibit a Colt six-shooter with markings on its yellowed buffalo-bone butt—several lines for killing bad men—two shorter ones for killing good men. According to Recoust, he had never been the first one to draw. Supposedly, in some cases, Recoust had been faster than his opponent. There was the time, he told, when he had shot Jim Corwell, the well-known gunman by the simple trick of confronting him when the man had the sun in his eyes. Another time he had challenged a notorious bad man to a drinking contest on a sizable bet. When finally Recoust claimed himself the winner, his totally drunk opponent had reached for his gun and a half-sober Recoust had shot him down. His stories were sometimes about famous desperados he claimed to have known, such as Doc Holiday, Wyatt Earp, Black Bart Boles and Frank Stillwell.

In his accounts, the cattle drives he had been on were mostly dangerous going over passes, across rapids or through the desert. Vivid and interesting, the tales seemed the product of a fertile imagination. The accounts made folks smile and sometimes laugh later in amusement. However, a cowboy background was vouched by his bowlegs. In the winter apart from the Christmas festivities, his stories were the only entertainment available so folks frequently sat around his warm stove. In the middle of snowstorms with the wind howling in the streets, one of the saloons or Recoust's store were the only refuges where you could spend some time. A story of how a bunch of desperados were held back by a cattle stampede or about the true worth of Helen Boulavier, the famous western courtesan, had a lot of allure.

Burgherton had been a serene town except for the time when the dang fool Dr. Morris had tried to talk the leading citizens into unneeded and expensive sewers when anybody could tell that all that was required were outhouses with holes in the ground. After recovering from a disastrous fire, the town had prospered and had acquired a hotel, three grist mills, a saw mill, an oil mill, a cotton factory, an iron factory, tanneries and two brothels. The latter nobody sober cared to mention except in a muted mumble. The serenity was broken when Joe Tollman came to town and his saloon became a meeting ground for unsavory characters. Nobody knew for sure whether Tollman was responsible, but some men made the rounds of businesses and asked the owners for money to insure their safety. Nobody took them seriously. After all, Burgherton wasn't Chicago. But then the Hotel Pleasant, the only hotel in town, had burned down and Sam Macemass, the owner of one of the saloons, was badly beaten. The police were unable to do anything. This was a totally new experience for which they were unprepared.

The unexpected and vicious happenings had everybody talking. Adam Recoust, of course, couldn't be silenced. There was only one way of handling such a situation, he claimed, and that was with a gun. Perhaps the fact that the whole town knew him, his loose talk and his colorful and innocuous status made him an obvious target.

Two men came into his store. It was early in the morning and the store was empty. Recoust wasn't immediately visible since he was in the storeroom in the back. "Hey, Grandpa," one of them yelled. Recoust stepped out with his peculiar bowlegged gait.

"What can I do for you, stranger?"

The two stocky strangers of indeterminate age looked menacing. "For only twenty dollars a month we can insure your store against accidents."

"What accidents?'

"You must have heard about the hotel fire and what happened to Mr. Macemass."

"Young fellah, there is nothing wrong with my hearing."

"We will collect the money on the first Monday of each month."

"There must be sompin' wrong with your hearing. I ain't said nothing."

The man who had remained silent leaned over and pushed a shelf so that all its contents fell to the ground.

"Don't be stupid Grandpa! Besides there are two of us."

Recoust laughed as he pulled out the six-shooter he must have had inside his belt, under his shirt.

"I got six bullets in this here gun."

It was difficult to take such an amusing and colorful old fellow seriously. The handgun looked more like a souvenir of the West rather than a weapon. As a way of response the silent man pulled at another shelf and the jars fell to the ground and shattered.

Recoust pressed the trigger six times and shot them both dead.

ADRIFT

Life sometimes is like being in fast moving rapids without oars and in a rudderless boat. As a child, Matt Ilbert would set free little paper boats into the stream not far from his family's home. There was no way of telling how far they could go before encountering an unexpected obstacle or an eddy that would tip and sink them. Many years later, this is how he felt about his own travails. He laughed at his own discomfort. After the votes had been counted, he had gone from anti-corruption candidate for the Assembly to a non-entity. His margin of loss had been substantial. Not surprisingly many thought he was too young while others thought he wasn't pompous enough, although they called it "being dignified."

His throat was still hurting from his perorations in rented halls and various churches. With some satisfaction he felt he had told no lies, although in some cases he had exaggerated a bit. He considered himself lucky to have been able to resist being dragged into a meaningless duel with his opponent. Although illegal, duels still took place in the first half of the nineteenth century. Refusing to honor a challenge was considered cowardly or an admission of being in the wrong. To no avail Matt had denied that he had sullied the reputation of his opponent's sister, Barbara De Witt. Not only he had never even mentioned her, his veiled reference to whoredom had been directed to the behavior of his opponent. He had even apologized for what he had actually not said. Apparently that wasn't enough. Albert De Witt's aim was apparently to either get rid of him or discredit him completely. The De Witts and the Iberts had held a grudge for generations. Matt doubted anybody remembered why, the facts having been obscured and distorted over the years. Naturally, Matt was adverse to putting his life in danger, but even more important he didn't like taking risks for no real reason. After a while he decided that being taken for a coward was the lesser of two evils.

The meeting in the rented hall, where he thanked the supporters of his unsuccessful political bid drew very few—perhaps a mere two dozen. Except for one, all were men. They were enthusiastic and urged him to try again. He was intrigued by the woman who had remained silent. Politics was considered the sole province of men. After all, women couldn't vote. She was rather pretty with regular features, chestnut hair and big expressive dark eyes. She dressed elegantly and in an obtrusive manner, making her presence seem even more improbable.

She lingered behind when the others left.

"Can I be of service?" he intoned, intrigued.

The look in her eyes was mischievous. "I was just checking on the current status of my chastity."

He felt himself blushing. "Barbara De Witt, I presume."

She laughed. "How did you guess?"

"Then, perhaps I can make amends for what I never said."

"How could you do that?"

"Would an ice cream do? There is a place on Broadway...."

She interrupted. "Isn't that a place where sweethearts and sometimes lovers meet?"

Matt was blushing again. He had never encountered rapier-like thrusts like hers. "Don't you think it would be appropriate?"

She laughed again, "I can't say yet."

He wasn't accustomed to flirtation and was surprised at their exchange. Usually, the only contact he had with women was in the form of very formal and dull conversations with a remarkable lack of success.

After the waiter had presented each one of them with a dish of ice cream, she was the first to speak.

"Aren't you afraid that this is a subterfuge for a De Witt to do away with an Ibert?"

"I haven't seen a stiletto, although I have been told that women's clothes can conceal anything."

She was suddenly serious. "Actually, I came to your meeting because you intrigue me and it's about time we stop this stupid fighting."

"As far as I'm concerned the grudge doesn't exist. But for some people I'm afraid it will last for a long time. You'd better tell me how I intrigue you. I'm bursting with curiosity and vanity! It better be good!"

She didn't deviate from the serious mood although she was smiling. "When you're not joking, you say what you mean and you mean what you say. Rare in politics, and usually fatal if you want to get elected."

The exchanges continued for a while and it was a pleasant interlude until they parted. Matt was not sure what kind of impression he had left. After all their exchanges had been about unimportant matters. He was glad to see that two persons on opposite sides of a divide could carry on a civil conversation. To top it off, she was very attractive—more because of her vivaciousness than her prettiness. During their conversation, he did reveal some of his inner self. With one phase of his life terminated, he was going to move upstate and see what opportunities existed there. No, he wasn't going to be a pioneer or start farming. Unfortunately the background of the Iberts was money—how to invest and how to make more. Just as bad as that of the De Witts! There were more interesting ways to live but they were unavailable to him.

At least a month later, he received a note signed only by her first name, he was puzzled. She wished to see him at the ice cream locale they had visited before. What did he have to lose? Besides, it was a welcome interruption from the arrangements he had to make for his trip. Obtaining letters of credit, letters of introduction and gathering information on how to travel, all had become a chore. An effort to obtain shares of companies doing business upstate also took some time. It required finding sellers of the appropriate papers after first evaluating their possible worth.

He waited for some time for her to appear, she came after his second order of lemonade. Although she looked the same—a well-dressed pretty woman—her manner had changed entirely. She was no longer the mischievous, fun-loving woman he had met before. A tenseness and determination in her manner, not there in their first meeting, was present.

"I'm glad to meet you again. Shall I order something for you?"

"No. I just want to talk."

"How can I be of service?"

"Well … I don't know exactly how to say it."

"With words, of course. There is no other way."

"It's not that simple. Words can misinform or be misunderstood." She continued after a pensive interval. "Perhaps it can only be said simply and directly. Will you take me with you when you leave?"

Matt was sure that his surprise and dismay registered on his face.

"I know, it sounds preposterous and I can't explain why I'm asking."

"Aside from inflaming the Ilbert-De Witt feud, I don't see what it would accomplish!"

"Please. It's nothing like that. I just can't tell you."

"Can't or won't?"

She blushed without answering. "A woman alone cannot travel easily. I promise you that I will not be a burden."

"If she travels with a man who isn't a relative she will be suspect. Even if I didn't besmirch your reputation before, travelling with me would really do it. And what is the point? I can't say yes without knowing more of what's in your mind. And what will you do when we reach the end of the line?"

"I really thought you might be more helpful. I had the impression that we were soul mates."

"Sorry, I think it would be a serious mistake."

She looked forlorn. It was a foolish notion, one of an immature child, that he knew she wasn't. He wondered what was behind her request. He was firm in his decision although he felt immense sympathy for her. Something horrendous must be driving her away.

Days later, when he was ready to travel and had supervised the loading of his luggage to the ship, she appeared at the dock. Dressed formally and somber, she pleaded again.

"Could you please talk to me one more time?"

He must have assented with a gesture because she continued.

"Please, let's go where we can be alone. I don't want to parade my problems in front of a crowd."

They stepped to the other end of the pier.

"Matt! Can I call you Matt?"

He bobbed his head.

"I'm sorry! This is very hard for me to tell." And after a pause. "You may not be aware that I'm only Albert's half sister ... and illegitimate at that. Very few people know that." After some silence. "I'm an embarrassment, now that he has reached some political prominence and his ambition has risen ... he wants to marry me off to a man I don't really know and who would be moving far away, I believe to Indiana. That would be an easy way to make me disappear. Please, please take me with you. I won't be a burden. I have some money and I don't mind working hard." Then with a smile, "You don't have to marry me or anything drastic like that. I'll go my own way."

"Why pick me?"

"I don't know very many men who are about to leave town and I trust you."

"We're not even friends."

"You're a friend as far as I'm concerned."

He felt as if he was about to make a serious mistake but couldn't help himself. His head motioning in the direction of the ship indicated his reluctant consent. His reward was a sigh of relief from the woman.

"I'll pay for the fare and you'd better have your stuff put next to mine."

She approached him and whispered. "I'm sorry. There is more to embarrass my brother. It might embarrass you as well. You see besides my birth, my mother was a woman of color. Not much of that, I think she was what they call an octoroon."

Matt smiled at her and touched her arm gently. "You're talking to Matt Ilbert, remember? No hidden complexities."

She again sighed with relief again.

❦   ❦   ❦

Troy, on the east side of the Hudson had been Matt's choice to settle down. The Erie Canal had just been opened to traffic in 1823, and with it opened up infinite possibilities for trading. Three ships regularly travelled between Troy and New York City, and several factories had been started in Troy. A steam ferry crossed the Hudson on a regular basis. Matt stayed at the Mansion House, a relatively new hotel. Barbara stayed in the same hotel for a few days, but then went her own way without leaving him a message.

As luck would have it, before leaving New York City he had picked up some shares of the Mohawk and Hudson Road to allow a railroad between Troy and Saratoga by the Rensselaer and Saratoga Railroad. Because the Troy group didn't have a majority interest and because of the rivalry between Albany and Troy for commercial routes, the deal proved very rewarding both in money and goodwill. Socially, however, his contribution helped him only marginally. He was invited to what were considered important occasions and his number of acquaintances was rather large but he had few true friends. As a bachelor he was considered a good catch but the number of women available was limited.

Barbara De Witt had kept her promise not to be a burden. He saw her once crossing the street. Troy was not a large town. She waved at him but made no attempt to contact him. He couldn't help wondering how she had fared. He eventually found out that she worked as a waitress in the hotel where they had stayed when they had first arrived. After a very fierce winter he became concerned about her welfare. The streets were not passable because of the snow and slush except by sleigh or snowshoes and the cold had been exceptional. He found her in a run-down boarding house. She hardly resembled the carefree woman he had first met or even the serious woman who wanted to travel with him. Her countenance showed worry and fatigue. She coughed fiercely just after she had come down from her room. Life is hard for a woman and twice as hard for a woman alone.

Matt acted on impulse and took her by the hand.

"Come with me. You're not in any shape to stay by yourself."

"Matt, I'll survive."

"You have to be alive to survive. Wrap yourself in everything warm that you have. I have a sleigh outside and some blankets and fortunately we don't have too far to go."

And that is how she came to live with him.

Matt had been able to take possession of a fairly large townhouse. Somehow he had graduated to having several servants. His business must be very lucrative, she concluded. She was not very demanding. The first week or two were spent in the bedroom assigned to her. Matt kept checking on her to her embarrassment. The meals—she could only accept soup in the first few days—were brought in by a servant, Millie. They had quickly become friends. Millie was her guide and contact to the outside.

Her cough had eventually stopped. Matt and Barbara started having their meals together. Barbara had regained some of her color. She ventured outside and she acquired the freedom of the town.

The spring announced itself with the breaking of the ice on the Hudson with a loud snap. Festivities followed for several days.

Barbara intercepted Matt before he was able to leave the house. She had regained her color and didn't look gaunt anymore.

"Matt, I should go my own way now."

"We have to talk some more. You should know all your possible alternatives. I don't want to have to rescue you again." He was sorry to have said that as soon as it left his mouth.

"What do you think my alternatives are?"

"Well, we could ignore the whole issue and you could live here indefinitely. As you might have guessed I'm doing quite well (knock on wood). I could probably set you up in some business. Perhaps a small store if you don't want to remain idle. I could remain as a silent partner. You could go back to New York City. Your brother might have recovered from his stupidity. When the Legislature is in session, he's just across the river in Albany, if you want to talk to him. Of course, you could always marry me if you choose a more conventional path."

The conversation had suddenly jolted her thoughts. The proposal was more of a joke than a request for marriage. But jokes sometimes have a way of acquiring an aura of reality. Was that something buried in the recondite folds of his mind? She certainly was very fond of him.

"Why would I want to marry you?"

"Because you like me, or at least used to like me and because I'm your friend."

His serious answer indicated to her that whatever was happening had escalated by several notches.

They married without much fanfare the following week.

❋   ❋   ❋

Barbara had known since she was very young where babies came from. In the happier days before her brother had tried to hide her, when her aunt had produced her little cousin, Barbara had heard the commotion, the rush to alert the midwife and the muted yells. She had quickly concluded that the process was protracted and involved pain.

What took place between husband and wife had been less clear. Until she was about fifteen she had thought only animals carried out such primitive goings-on. Her friend Alice had laughed at her naivety and quickly informed her of how wrong she was.

Barbara got accustomed to Matt's clumsy love-making. At first it was just like fulfilling a bodily function. Then Matt became less clumsy, he no longer placed his whole weight on her, and then he became more skillful. She found the process had become enjoyable.

The morning sickness was almost welcome, as unpleasant as it was. She loved the idea of having a human being forming inside her. A human being to love without reservation. Matt also seemed very pleased, possibly because it confirmed his masculinity. Men were such little boys about so many things, she thought.

The birth process might have been a repeat of her aunt's experience. A midwife was quickly summoned when the contractions became frequent. Millie was also present. The midwife chased Matt away. In her experience men were just a nuisance. The physical effort and the pain covered Barabara with sweat. It took a long time but then somehow it was all over and she heard the muted cries of a new baby. Once cleaned up, the little girl looked wrinkled and dark but still beautiful. How could somebody so small be so perfect and so beautiful?

Barbara had heard that many women were depressed after a birth. Instead, somehow, she felt elated. Matt was allowed in the room. To her surprise tears were streaking his face.

All he could say was: "I'm so happy! So happy!" After a while he had more to say, "I was so scared something would go wrong. And that's the prettiest baby in the whole world!"

Millie lifted the baby and handed her to him and he cradled the little girl in his arms.

"Matt, do you love me?" Barbara had never heard him say it.

"Oh, Barbara. How could you doubt it? I fell in love with you the moment I first met you. How could you possibly think I would marry somebody I didn't love?" Barbara knew that it had happened to many couples. She was just exultant that he loved her now. Of that she was sure. She wasn't ready to accept that he had fallen in love when he had first met her. Her feelings for him until that moment were more those of trust and hope than love. After his declaration, she suddenly realized she loved him and their little baby deeply and irrevocably. She was filled by a warm feeling. She was very happy and contended despite all the physical discomforts and her sore breasts.

Life sometimes is like being in fast moving rapids without oars and in a rudderless boat but then sometimes it leads you to the right place.

ZIA CONCETTA

You must have read in the papers of the weird outdated Sicilian custom of forcing marriage on a young woman via an arranged rape by a suitor considered suitable by her family. This is done with the consent of the family, presumably to let the girl see the light of reason. The idea is that no other man would want the deflowered woman, so the poor victim has to capitulate through necessity. Supposedly, a woman is not able to survive on her own. Well, as you might have also read, a woman a few years ago defied the custom and eventually married somebody other than the selected suitor.

I was told that my Aunt Concetta, eventually the mother of four, had gone through the same cruel ritual many years before. Or to be more accurate, it's what I pasted together from hints, bits and pieces, veiled references and deep sighs. Family secrets are not divulged readily. I had never heard the story before, not surprisingly since I had left with my parents at a tender age. The source of the account was primarily my cousin Roberta, Concetta's daughter, when I visited the island after three decades of absence in the States. Roberta looks much like me, not unexpectedly since my mother is Concetta's older sister. Pleasantly plum, with dark looks and gray hair, Roberta has unexpected flashes of energy and temper.

After getting the first hint, I had to entreat and cajole. I imagine one reason I was given answers at all was, in part, to show me how out of touch with reality I have been, spoiled by American largess and naivete. On other occasions, Roberta's tale was liberally supplemented by many hints and murmurs from other family members. I'm not quite sure of some of the details, Roberta didn't want to be too explicit even if she was talking woman to woman and some of her story resembled a parable rather than a straight narrative. On top of that, she got so excited at crucial points in her account that she would break into dialect, which after all these years, I have trouble dealing with. But this is what

I understood. Keep in mind that the Maletti women are known for their powerful curses and the outcome was quite different from the traditional or even the more recent breaches of tradition.

Concetta was a beautiful and somewhat spoiled young woman. When still a young girl, her family treated her much like a boy and she even had dabbled in the tool and die machine shop of her father—as if a woman were suited for such work! Somewhat of a tomboy before acquiring her feminine allures, she had been known to have a mind of her own. Later, her fine light complexion, curvaceous body, raven hair and expressive dark eyes had set many male hearts aflutter. Such attributes represented a serious responsibility to the family who had to make sure that no natural impulses would put her nubile state in jeopardy. Marriage to a respectable, wealthy and important man seemed to be the easiest way of taking care of such a delicate situation. Ezio Dolimiti was interested in Concetta's charms and had formally contacted Concetta's parents. Concetta had treated him politely but coldly even before he had expressed an interest. He came from a wealthy family—handsome and dashing, he cut an attractive figure. Although he was rumored to be somewhat wild, particularly in relation to obstreperous parties and women, he surely would settle down once he had the responsibility of marriage and children. Concetta refused to even consider marriage to him.

One day, to her surprise, Concetta was left alone in the house. This had never happened before. Dolimiti rang the bell and upon being admitted into the house, tried to sweet talk his way into her graces. When this didn't seem to work, he started to force himself on her. The initial rejected passionate kisses were followed by more intimate attempts to disrobe her.

"You'd better stop that right now! Or you'll have to face my family."

"Little girl, you shouldn't be so silly. Many are the women who would envy you. And, do you think I would be here if your parents didn't know and approve?"

"If you wrong me so miserably, my *maledizione* will follow you and you'll wish you had died first."

Dolmitti laughed at this and forced himself on her. She struggled, but the man was too strong for her. Absurdly, he whispered endearments into her ear. The process was even more unpleasant than she had imagined. Later, she tearfully confided to her parents what had happened but received no sympathy.

A family meeting to discuss the matter was quickly assembled the following day, with Ezio Dolmitti present. Her parents and two sets of uncles, aunts and older cousins had conferred and were all present. Concetta's father, my grandfather, summarized for her the prevailing opinion.

"We are sorry for the unpleasantness. What happened is only natural during courtship. We know what's best for you. You'll have to marry Ezio. You'll see that Ezio will make you happy. There is no other possible recourse."

Throughout this admonishment, Dolmitti had a triumphant smile on his face.

Unfortunately, they hadn't taken into consideration Concetta's personality. She spoke clearly and deliberately.

"I really don't understand what you're saying. Unfortunately, the poor man is incapable." At this point Concetta blushed demurely. "I don't know how an innocent girl can tell you without being deeply embarrassed … He is what you might call flaccid." She continued with tears in her eyes. "I'm still intact … all you have to do is look at the bed sheet, not even a drop of blood. You put me through all that unpleasantness for nothing." And then in a firmer, sad tone, "I'll never forgive you."

Ezio was besides himself with humiliation and fury. He exclaimed, "Lying slut," followed by obscenities no person from a good family would ever use. He couldn't stand the inquiring and disapproving looks of the family. He left. The family was dumfounded and their exchanges became a confused buzzing.

Still furious, Ezio suddenly came back with a pistol. Fear froze everybody in place as if they were pausing for a photograph. He pressed the trigger in order to pepper the unfortunate Maletti family with bullets. But that must be when Concetta's curse came into play. The gun exploded and he lost his right hand and one eye. Fortunately, *Pronto Soccorso* was quickly summoned to take care of the unfortunate man or it might have been much worse.

I have no idea how such distressing events could have happened to Ezio Dolmitti. Concetta's account could have been correct. However, bed sheets, of course, can be changed and it wouldn't take much to obstruct the muzzle of a gun. But these are only conjectures. I simply understand that these happenings took place. How, I cannot tell you for sure.

MEANDERING

Ads had been placed throughout the country in newspapers to find a man born on February 25 who had been given up for adoption as a newborn twenty-eight years before. The lawyers hired by Edwin Lawrence, the man responsible for the ads, had screened a variety of claimants. The fancy that it might lead to a financial reward had attracted a number of men who did not conform with the requirements. Some of them had the appropriate birth date but their adoption could not be documented adequately. Others had produced birth certificates that did not belong to them.

Jennifer, Edwin's daughter, had been persuaded to check the three finalists who might be the genuine article. She consented to these interviews reluctantly, out of respect for her father. As young as she was, she had been trained as a lawyer and was recognized by all her friends and acquaintances for her perspicacity. The need to find Ed's biological son escaped her. Why chase ghosts? The lawyers who had organized the search had rented rooms in a fancy hotel. Trust lawyers to devise complex and expensive maneuvers, thought Jenny, who for good reason didn't respect members of her own profession. She had faced them often enough at the conference table or in the courtroom. Paul Robinson was the last man she had to interview. When the query had been carried by *The Chronicle,* Philip Robinson, Paul's father, had seen it and thought Paul should present himself.

So far the search had been a complete waste of time, she was sure. The two men she had already interviewed were convincing but bore no physical resemblance to her father. Had there been any doubt, a DNA test would have been used to solve any possible indecision. Why bother with one more interview? She hesitated before entering the room, then tucked the folder with the appropriate information under her arm and opened the door without knocking. The sitting room was like the others she had seen in the hotel—bright and with cutesy prints of Monmartre, thick wall-to-wall carpeting, several upholstered chairs and a view of the teaming city through the window.

Seeing Paul fidgeting in one of the chairs, a cold frisson coursed her very being. Although much younger, he was the image of her father, Edwin Lawrence. Even sitting he was clearly tall, with cold blue eyes but with auburn hair where Ed's was mostly gray. He was dressed casually. In the fancy hotel environment it might have been a statement. She forced herself to keep emotions out of her voice.

"I'm Jennifer Lawrence." She shook his hand as he got up.

"Pleased to meet you—I think." They sat down and after a moment of silence. "Let's get this show on the road."

She smiled, hoping that it was a cold smile. "You don't want to be here?"

"Well, it's too complicated to explain. I'm doing this because my dad wants me to."

"Well, you can leave any time you want. I'll try to go through the paces and if you're interested in our conclusions we'll let you know. I believe you have two younger sisters. Not adopted. Apparently there was no problem conceiving. Isn't it unusual to adopt a child before trying to have your own?"

Paul sounded annoyed. "You'll have to ask my parents or some sociologist. I have no idea."

She shuffled through the folder one of the lawyers had given her. "It says here that you're unemployed."

Paul laughed. "That's why I'm here. My dad thinks that I need to reconstruct my life in some unspecified way. He thinks that my present idleness and lack of direction are not healthy and wants to interest me in something." Actually, he was spending much of his time in the library, doing some research and trying to write what he could conclude from his war experience. Frequently painful to recall and write, when put into words, the accounts seemed melodramatic and at other times banal. They never seemed to strike the right note without sounding false and he was never able to express the horror that filled him even though he hadn't had first hand experience with some of the dramatic happenings. His savings and a surprising but modest advance from a publisher allowed him to keep body and soul together.

Paul noted that the woman talking to him was rather attractive—lovely complexion and a face if not beautiful, interesting. Her severe but fashionable business suit, was meant to convey that this was just business, he thought. Her attractiveness irritated him even more. Just what he needed, he thought sarcastically. To be interviewed by a bimbo for no particular reason—some relative or parents searching for a son they had abandoned. Or had the search been initiated by a woman? Mothers seemed to have second thoughts more frequently, although a wait of twenty-eight years seemed unlikely.

Jenny continued, "You're recovering from something?"

"Not that I know of. But you know a stint in war and working on difficult translations for the government takes its toll."

The material in the folder had spelled out that he had been with the Special Forces in Afghanistan and had been chosen to translate for the CIA because of a knowledge of Arabic languages.

"So you were in that war. What about your association with the CIA?"

"They got me as a translator when the Iraq thing came up. Arabic languages is one of my things."

"How did you acquire that? Isn't it unusual?"

"You may have noticed that my dad is a professor specializing in the history of the Middle East and Northern Africa. He had to cultivate those languages. When I was in my teens, he passed some of his enthusiasm onto me."

"Is that what they speak in Afghanistan?"

"No, they speak Pashtun, Dari and some Turkic languages. I had no language advantage when serving there."

"What happened in your CIA job?"

"Some people mistake disagreement with disloyalty. That's what is wrong with this country. I was fired. But what has this to do with your quest?"

She avoided responding. "Do you know anything about when you were adopted and why your biological parents wanted to give you up?"

"They don't give you that kind of information and frankly I don't care. I'm pretty happy with my family. I've never been self-conscious about being adopted. Sure, I have known the facts for years but I've been the older brother of two young girls for a long time. I was always treated with overwhelming affection by parents and siblings. Of course it is a bit different now. I don't live with them and one of my sisters is in college. But then or now, my biological origins have never seemed important."

Jennifer was irritated to say the least. She didn't like his attitude and the fact that it made her efforts pretty useless. Paul's barely veiled antagonism didn't bode well. She was certain that this man was her brother but that discovery was not likely to lead to anything useful for the welfare of Edwin Lawrence.

"Well, if you are the man we are searching for there are some advantages in knowing the bare facts. Some are medical, such as parents' health history. Thank you for contacting us."

She was on her feet again and they shook hands on parting. She knew a little about the baby's adoption and would have felt better if the whole matter had been left alone. She went to a conference room to summarize her three interviews for the two lawyers. She didn't care for the two humorless men in well-cut somber suits and colorful power ties. There didn't seem to be much point in talking to them. Paul was certainly the man they had been searching for. Without sitting down, she communicated her conclusion in few words and resisted their entreaties to stay to discuss matters further.

Stepping out of the elevator into the large lounge with a bar at one end, she saw Paul at a distance sitting at a table with a drink in front of him. She needed a stiff drink too. Suddenly, she sympathized with his ordeal and approached the table.

"Could we talk some more? … Socially this time."

She liked his relaxed smile which she hadn't seen before.

"Why not?"

She sat down across from him. "Perhaps I can tell you some facts that might be useful. I wasn't completely frank. I'm sorry. Edwin Lawrence is a nice man. If he wants to find you, there must be a good reason. I'm not in a position to pass judgment. When he gave you up, he was broke, terribly sick and confused. His wife, your biological mother, had just died at your birth. It took him a few years to recover. Ed married my mom a few years later. She was a single mother also widowed with one child, namely me. I was a very young girl when they got married. Ed is the only dad I can remember clearly. He has been good to me. I love him. I don't know why he's looking for you. All I know is that he'll contact you. Facing an unknown past might bother you, but don't think he wants to make demands or trouble you with false sentimentality. He's a very kind man. Do what you think is best for you, but if you agree to meet him, please be kind." She looked up and smiled at the waitress and ordered a gin and tonic.

They sat in companionable silence. Paul concluded that she wasn't at all like he'd thought from their meeting. There was a good deal to like.

He smiled at her and said, "Thank you." They sat silently sipping their drinks and then shook hands and parted, Paul remaining at the table.

Paul went to see Edwin Lawrence after all. His dad had pushed him in that direction, "Haven't you ever wondered about your biological parents? Apparently, lots of adopted children do."

"Look, you are my father and Sophie is my mother and that's all there is to it."

"Oh, I know you feel that way. But there are also some advantages in knowing the bare facts. Some are medical, such as a family health history. And you never know when some of the hidden realities might haunt you. It's best to face them before you are bothered by them and not wait until the time when for some reason you might be more vulnerable. We all have our downs. Meeting with Lawrence will put a period on some questions."

"The voice of reason speaks again."

"Again, the young condescend to the old and wise!"

"Something like that," said Paul with a smile.

For his visit, Paul made sure he was dressed informally but in decent clothing. His cotton pants still had a crease in them and he had put on a clean short-sleeved shirt. Lawrence's house was in a fashionable district of the city, between city and suburb. He had no trouble getting there with his clunker. When he finally spotted the house, he was amused by the contrast between his car and the BMW and Porsche resting on the driveway. Alighting from his car, he admired the house. It was one of those luxurious structures in which each room seems to be filled with light as if it were part of the outdoors, the well wooded and well tended grounds. He hesitated for an instant before pressing the bell.

The wait was short. Jennifer Lawrence opened the door with a radiant smile. She didn't look at all like the woman who had interviewed him—the severity and wariness were gone. She was dressed informally—blue jeans and t-shirt.

"Welcome. I'm glad you decided to come after all!" She led him to the garden in the back. Shade trees had sculptured a nook out of its surroundings.

There was an outdoor table surrounded by four chairs. The tall old man sitting there got up. Half-hidden tears shined in his eyes. It was a clumsy moment for the both of them. They shook hands and it was the older man who broke the silence.

"We have a few things to talk about. There is no hurry. Can I offer you a drink? It's a hot day." When he saw Paul's hesitation, he addressed himself to Jennifer who was hovering protectively in the background. "Could you bring us some lemonade please? And come sit with us, please."

Although Jenny's presence somehow helped, the ice cold lemonade pleasant as it was did nothing to allay the awkwardness. After they had been sitting for a while, words came pouring out of Ed Lawrence.

"When I lost you it was the worst period of my life. It has been tormenting me for years. I know you've been very happy with your adopted family and that helps me face my past." But he still wanted to put an end to that torment and couldn't see how he could do it without meeting Paul. In fact, he suggested shyly, perhaps they could meet and talk once a week, perhaps for dinner, just the two of them.

That's what they did for some time. As Paul learned a little bit at a time after each visit, he was making the acquaintance of a very good man. Paul found that he liked Edwin Lawrence, although he had no strong feelings for him. How could he?

At times, Paul wasn't sure what Ed Lawrence was trying to say. "I haven't told you the whole story and perhaps I don't understand it too well myself. I feel some foreboding as if I am running out of time. Before anything happens, I want to make sure that my life is completed. For that reason I had to find you. I don't know how to explain what I feel. It's probably my imagination and advancing old age. For one thing, there are some irregularities in my company that I don't understand and which will have to be rooted out. But I don't want to burden you with my problems."

Paul didn't know what to think about these revelations but he had great respect for intuition. It had saved his life more than once during his war years.

Jenny's initiative brought a new period. She organized a picnic in the same backyard where Paul had first met Ed Lawrence. The mood was definitely festive. Paul's parents, Philip and Sophie, and one of Paul's two sisters, Alice, met Martha and Edwin Lawrence, for the first time. Ellen, Paul's absent sister, was away at college. Jenny's fiancé, Hugh Stewart, hadn't been able to free himself from his commitments, Jenny explained after pulling Paul aside.

"George, my cousin, the son of Ed's brother, isn't here either. I invited him too. He's still in a snit from the time Dad and Mom got married fifteen years ago! Until then he had been treated like an only child. Can you imagine? A man in his late thirties still in a snit about nothing. Unearthing one more sibling probably pleased him even less! To top it off, he works for Dad and probably dreams that his position there is threatened by me!"

Paul couldn't help notice that Jenny cleverly and good-naturedly intervened here and there, introducing, making sure that the exchanges were meaningful. He marveled at her firmness and kindness. The two older women and the two dads seemed to hit it off. They had so much in common! Alice, although much younger than Jenny, seemed to be particularly impressed with her and made sure never to be too far from her. They seemed to be more like sisters than two

young women who had just met. Paul heard a snatch of their conversation—the idea that there might be some logic in taking a year off before college
to explore the world. That's what Jenny had done, except that she had worked
first for a full year. She had felt that there would be more enjoyment if she
earned the wherewithal for her adventures. Alice seemed to appreciate the sentiment.

Jenny offered to serve as a guide through the house and the small group
traipsed through the various rooms. Elegance and neatness seemed to be the
rule. She stopped at one of the bedrooms.

"This used to be my room. I still use it when I choose to stay overnight. As
you can see it has Hugh's picture on display. Isn't he handsome? I have a better
one in my apartment. We are getting married in another month and I will have
to move again."

Hugh appeared to Paul to look like a movie star, more attractive than any
man should be allowed to be, he thought.

Jenny worked in the Child Protection Agency not too far from the library
that Paul favored for his writing and research. She explained that the Agency
was a private group which helped Social Services and frequently offered tem-
porary refuge for abused children, not to mention initiating court actions or
supporting motions as friends of the court. The two of them found it conve-
nient to occasionally have lunch together. Paul had mixed feelings about her.
Here was a woman he could become interested in and she turned out to be his
sister! The fact that she was engaged further vexed him. But there was much to
like about her. Without artifice, she had a warm personality. Her interest in the
people around her was genuine and appealing.

After a while, Paul found the various facets of her nature fascinating. Once
he picked her up at her apartment and she spent some time with the doorman
exchanging accolades about the weather. With Paul, most of the time she
laughed a lot. The world was a mass of contradictions and drolleries. As a
lunch companion she was interesting and pleasant. She spoke as if she had
known Paul forever. She could be in earnest as well—mostly, when it had to do
with her work. She spoke about children who had been treated cruelly. How
laws were insufficient protection because the funds assigned for enforcement
were always insufficient. That's when the Child Protection Agency came in.

She didn't avoid any personal topic and even spoke about her fiancé. She
regretted spending only weekends with him. Their situation was a departure
from the current practice, Paul had heard about: couples living together for a
while before marriage.

For his part, Paul found himself revealing events that had been buried in the recondite corners of his mind. He had never spoken to anybody about his writing and account of his war experience. His disclosure was received with sympathy and interest. Jenny insisted on reading at least part of it. A few days later when they got together again, he couldn't miss the affectionate and concerned look in her eyes.

"Paul," she commented, "you certainly went through hell. You're wrong in your judgement about the writing. There is nothing melodramatic or banal about it. There is horror and a reflection of the contrasting boredom of the times in-between. I find it a very sensitive account. Parts are upsetting to the reader but so must be any naked reality of war."

When he expressed an interest in seeing where she worked, she took him to the Child Protection Agency on a floor set aside for the pursuits of several members of the group. As he understood, most of the time each of the colleagues worked independently. They all looked up as the two of them entered. Paul guessed the average age of the group was about thirty, except for a middle-aged man, Jake Robertson. Robertson was out of place among the casually dressed youths. Bald, graying and dressed in a suit and tie he seemed to have stepped out of an ad for a banking or insurance concern.

Just after Paul was introduced, Robertson spoke up.

"Nice to meet you. You must be a relative."

"Something like that."

"Jenny is a wonderful girl ... Pardon me! Woman! You must know that side of her well. But there is a side of Jenny I bet you don't know. We call her "the pit bull." Wouldn't think a nickname like that could apply to such a sweet and pretty girl, but it's very apt." And after Paul smiled amused. "Once she goes after a cause or a case she never lets go. Neither snow, nor rain, nor gloom of night ... On top of it she's afraid of nothing. Politics and threats don't faze her in the least. She just tackled, along with his cadre of highly paid lawyers, no less than John Overbecker, the billionaire, the fifty-year-old juvenile delinquent. And he lost custody of his son!"

Although Jenny knew that he wasn't trying to embarrass her she blushed. Robertson's praises were sincere. However, she felt she had to retaliate.

"Somebody has to do his or her job rather than sit around and gossip."

The man chuckled, "Touché, touché!" and looking at Paul, "But take my word, she's awesome!"

Paul had found that something had fundamentally changed in him since he had gotten to know Jenny. In his mind, the present seemed to have gained a greater draw than the war, tragedy and gore of his fading obsessions. Her stories about the Child Protection Agency had found a response deep in him. The service had custody of abused or abandoned children, supposedly temporarily, although many had been there for some time. He had volunteered to help. Not everybody was allowed into what its keepers regarded the sanctuary, but Jenny's recommendation had opened the door for him.

He showed up, with some trepidation. What did he know about children? But even the first visit drew him in emotionally. The woman who accompanied him into the playroom, Martha Zim, was younger than he expected. She might have been his own age. She was dressed in jeans and a sweat shirt with the logo of the organization. He had been warned about how to dress and he wore a similar attire.

"I'm going to take you where the youngest group is now. Not the babies and toddlers. Those present an entirely different problem. Don't fret. You'll see what they need. Just be there. They are starved for attention even though we have several volunteers and staff members who spend time with them."

The handful of boys and girls in the playroom looked at him with reserve and suspicion. Martha Zim introduced Paul as a friend who had come to keep them company. A serious boy of about three riveted his big brown eyes on him. Then finally, he seemed to make up his mind.

"Daddy! Daddy!" All Paul had to do was to go down on his hunches and open his arms to receive the young charmer.

Once the ice was broken, several children crowded around him. After that he organized games, read children's books and told stories. Paul was then expected to show up at least twice a week. His donation of a train set became one of the favorite toys. He tried to have a highly organized play. But it was hard to prevent the various pieces from dispersing around the room.

Eventually, Jenny took him to meet her fiancé, Hugh. Paul could have done without that visit but it was one of the necessary consequences of his contact with Jenny. Hugh met them at his place of work—an investment concern. He was going through a very busy period as he as trying to clear the deck before the wedding.

In Paul's eyes, he looked like a perfectly suited banker, at least one shown in the television ads. Respectability, tradition, reliability, wealth, all rolled into one. Hugh was friendly, kissed Jenny briefly and shook hands with Paul with a brilliant smile.

"I've heard a lot about you," he volunteered.

The conversation was short and sterile. Paul had a hard time explaining to himself why he disliked Hugh. Was it because he was a success, his exact opposite? Or was Paul a bit jealous because of his relationship with Jenny?

❀   ❀   ❀

Maintaining himself physically—not just his musculature but also cultivating quick physical responses—was a habit Paul found necessary for his wellbeing. None of these skills were needed in his new life. Perhaps they were important for his self-respect. Perhaps the central idea in judo—being responsible for the defeat as well as the welfare of his opponent—appealed to him. Paul had been able to secure space for their practice in the Athletic Club.

Akimura was a master with no clear roots in the various clubs where martial arts were practiced, although he was probably the highest ranking judo black-belt in the city. He liked to teach and work out with Paul to avoid the public eye. Sometimes, perhaps in one encounter out of ten, Paul had been able to throw the master. He was rewarded by the man lying down on the mat laughing uproariously. Paul often wondered whether Aki was allowing his occasional success.

Sometimes Aki would bring some other worthy opponent to allow Paul to hone his skills. Or as Aki put it, to teach him humility, which unfortunately was often the case, which meant being slammed unexpectedly and unceremoniously onto the mat.

After an intense work out and a shower, Paul was reluctant to abandon the comradery. "Let's get a drink, Aki."

"Okay, but I have to get home soon."

As they sat at a table in the club's bar, Paul ordered a beer, Aki a Sprite. He explained, "My wife doesn't want me to drink."

Paul wondered why a cold beer tasted twice as good after having exercised to exhaustion. It was then that he heard his name.

"Paul. Paul Robinson! Isn't it?"

Paul turned. It was a voice from the past, from his college days. "Charlie Cornwell, I'll be damned! What are you doing here?"

"Just visiting from Detroit. Attending a congress."

"But why are you in this egregious facility?"

"A special deal, thank God. I have to tend to my abs! Even a few days can mess your regimen."

"Oh! Excuse me, this is Mr. Akimura. An old friend from college, Charlie Cornwell."

"Please to meet you, Mr. Cornwell." And the two shook hands.

"But, Paul I really have to leave. My wife expects me home." Aki left behind two bills ignoring Paul's gesture intended to mean that he would take care of it.

It was an opportunity to catch up on the events of the past years. "Did you marry Bess?"

"Sure, married five years ago. Just divorced. Two kids." For reasons that he couldn't define, Paul felt saddened. He had liked Bess. At one time, he had even dated her. Charlie continued. "That's the best part, the kids I mean, even if I don't see them too often. And you! Did you ever marry? To tell you the truth, I thought you had died!"

"I didn't get married and I imagine lots of people wish my demise to have actually happened. A long time ago, I told you it would take a platinum bullet to get me! The Taliban didn't understand that they needed that metal." Paul had no intention of discussing the real events in his life. Charlie guffawed, and continued, "I'm with a bunch of guys who are going to hit the high spots tonight. Why don't you come with us?"

Paul couldn't think of a worse way of spending an evening but he demurred unable to think of an excuse. The tug to please an old acquaintance was undeniable. "I'll accompany you for old time's sake seeing as this is my hometown, but only if you don't mention past or future deaths."

"It's a deal."

Well aware that he hadn't fully recovered, Paul hoped nobody would speak about the war—either the one in Afghanistan or the present one. Does one ever get over a war and forget the dying and the suffering? He was prepared to be quite rude if anybody opened his mouth on one of those topics.

The group found itself at the "Martini"—a nightclub which had become popular lately. Paul hadn't been in a nightclub in years and didn't know what to expect. When they entered, an attractive woman with a sultry voice and courageously exposed shoulders and cleavage in a fashionable gown was conjuring a love song while illuminated by the spotlight. Paul found her attractiveness pleasing. He was surprised at the quality of her singing and enjoyed her performance thoroughly. Soon he had a beer in front of him. His companions choices were more varied, from martinis to margueritas to plain old-fashioned scotch on the rocks. The men he was with were very much like Charlie—charming, quick witted, boisterous and of very little substance as far as Paul could tell from the limited exposure. They were there to enjoy themselves.

Paul had been swept along by a past he hardly remembered. Years before, he must have been much like his nightclub companions, but for him those days were gone.

Although the background light was dim, his eyes quickly got accustomed to the semi-darkness. For some reason his attention was attracted by a couple at a nearby table. The man and a very attractive woman were nuzzling. The woman was wearing one of the revealing dresses that left a good deal of the breasts bared as seemed to be the fashion. The man bent down and kissed the part of the breasts left exposed. The woman giggled appreciatively.

Suddenly, Paul couldn't get over the impression that he knew the man. Was that Hugh Stewart, Jenny's fiancé? He certainly looked like him. A little later, the man must have taken another liberty, as Paul heard the woman exclaim amusedly, "Not here Hugh!"

Paul was sufficiently disturbed to leave the group with apologies as soon as he had finished his drink.

Maybe it wasn't at all what he thought. Mores had changed since he had come back into the real world! But then maybe it was exactly what he thought—the man was cheating on Jenny. And what could Paul do about it?

He suddenly felt he was in a ridiculous and tenuous position. Shouldn't he do something? Poor Jenny might be approaching a precipice and deserved a warning. But what could he do? What could he say? "As your brother, a man who is falling for you in small steps, I have to tell you your fiancé is cheating on you." Perhaps he should speak to her parents. They might know what to do to soften the blow and do it kindly—as if betrayal ever could be softened with kindness.

Events caught up with him, however, and action on his part would have to be delayed.

Paul didn't realize how distressed he was about what he had witnessed. Jenny had called him on the phone the following morning.

"How about lunch tomorrow?"

Paul felt a stab of concern but could hardly object to her proposal. They were to meet in a downtown restaurant with ample parking underground. For a change, Jenny's work had taken her out of the office and she had to drive to arrive there.

At lunch their interactions were strained. Paul found he just didn't have the courage to disrupt her complacency. It had become hard to find a topic to talk about. Jenny felt the unspoken tension and voiced her puzzlement. "I don't know what's the matter, but something is bothering you."

From the restaurant, they headed for the basement garage. Although distracted by his own concern, Paul hadn't lost his habit of noticing everything around him. There were several people heading down the stairs. A man was following them closely down the cement steps. There was no reason to be suspicious of his behavior. Paul's alarm had no real basis. Nevertheless, he felt something was out of place. Was it a remnant of paranoia left over from his past experiences? At a sharp turn of the stairs, for an instant, the space was only occupied by the three of them. The man was close, perhaps closer than what one would have expected. Suddenly turning, Paul was faced with a handgun with silencer being levelled at Jenny. Instinctively, he quickly caught and twisted the gun to one side. The ping of a bullet from the dislodged gun hit the stairs. Then, he found himself lifting the man and dumping him down the stairs headfirst. His response had been closer to his early Special Forces' training, in a throw that Aki would not have approved of.

Confused and pale, Jenny had trouble meeting his eyes.

"I couldn't help it, Jenny! Please don't look. It's horrible." And then he stepped down to where the inert body was laying. The would be killer was quite dead possibly by a broken neck.

Paul was reluctant to leave the scene until the police were called in. "Somebody call 911, please!" he yelled.

At the police station, his story had to be repeated several times. Jenny, distressed, really didn't understand much of what had happened. Paul was afraid that the event, horrible as it was, had created a chiasm between them.

That his story, as unlikely as it sounded, was immediately accepted surprised Paul. The investigation seemed to be headed by Lieutenant Gross. Bald, somewhat chubby, he looked like a cautious, unambitious fellow except for two piercing eyes that reflected an enquiring, prodding mind.

"Any idea of who was the primary target? There were two of you. It's most likely that eventually he would have wanted to kill both of you so as not to leave a witness."

"What a happy thought! My feeling is that Ms. Lawrence was the target. That's what I thought I saw, but I might be wrong. I have kept a low profile since I returned from D.C., so I'm unlikely to have even attracted attention."

As it soon became obvious, the police believed his account. The fact that the dead stranger had no identification and his possession of a handgun of low caliber with a silencer suggested the would-be assassin was a hit man. Furthermore, Gross told him later, unsolved murders with the same pattern had occurred in other parts of the country.

As distraught as she had been at first, Jenny seemed to calm down as the matter was discussed. Paul was relieved that she looked at him without a trace of fear or concern. He had been afraid the unpleasant experience and his role in it might have destroyed the comradery and affection that held them together.

Over Jenny's protest, the police assigned a policewoman to accompany her for her protection.

A later visit by Paul alone to the police station framed their options. On his previous excursion into the police station, Paul and Jenny had been interrogated in a conference room. On his second visit, after he was summoned, Paul found himself in a large room sitting at Gross's desk. Around them were battered desks, plainclothes policemen manning some of them, phones ringing and the atmosphere of tedious routine. Gross spoke first.

"I'm sure you were right, Ms. Lawrence must have been the intended target. We have concluded that the dead man was a professional hit man. He had the misfortune not to realize that you were present. A hit man costs money. I have a list of all the cases Ms. Lawrence has been involved in. There are only two that stand out. One involves Mario Ruggero and the other is the case of John Overbecker. Ruggero is a minor hoodlum who abused his wife and children. Ms. Lawrence was merciless. He came out looking like a cowardly bully who just happened to have good lawyers. Although she failed in removing his children from under his roof, she'd damaged his credibility and the notion of manhood among the set of people he deals with. He may well have wanted to get even. However, I would have expected him to use some local talent. The gunman was definitely not local. Overbecker deserves scrutiny. He lost custody of his son. He's very rich although his contacts with the appropriate murderous set must be very limited."

After a short interruption he continued. "If we were dealing with Ruggero, it would be easy to get a warrant to tap his phones. He's involved in so many illicit activities! But a rich man with a retinue of lawyers is harder to get at. I figure that he would have found it hard to find a hit man unless one of his lawyers is really bent. Let's assume it isn't so. What would you do? Cruising the local bars to find a gun for hire has gotten many would-be murders into trouble. He couldn't be that stupid, although one never knows!"

Paul had a suggestion. "I don't know if it would work but I presume he could have read the ads in 'Soldier of Fortune.' Something not too obvious but offering super confidential services."

"You're exactly right. We can repeat the process. Once we can identify the man and show a likely intent to commit a crime, we can get a warrant. And you have the appropriate background. Many men looking for action were trained during the Gulf War or have Special Forces training. And your connection to Jennifer Lawrence is not well known. Once you're contacted, we can tap his fucking phones."

"I see you looked into my past! But wouldn't I be the wrong person?"

"You mean because you're involved with her? In my book precisely because you are involved with her. Wouldn't you take risks for her safety?"

"I would risk my life for her."

"Oh! That's a bit excessive. We are only hoping for your cooperation. You must be in love with her. But that doesn't really make sense does it?"

"Yes, I'm afraid that's what it means. And we are not really brother and sister. We have different parents. Whether she'll accept that is another matter. But that doesn't have to concern you." Paul had had no idea he felt that strongly. His spontaneous declaration had come out without reflection.

He had arranged with Gross to be alerted if anything unusual confronted Jenny, even if unrelated to her safety. The telephone call came from Sargent Ramirez, the police woman who had been assigned to escort Jenny.

"Mr. Robinson, you'd better come. I don't know what to do. Something happened. Not a police matter, but I don't know how to handle it. We are at Ms. Lawrence's apartment."

Upon his arrival, Jenny in tears flew into his arms. His first thought was entirely selfish. "She's still fond of me. I haven't alienated her after all." This was followed by a stab of concern for her.

"Oh God, Paul. Thank you for coming."

She stayed in his arms until she could collect her thoughts. "We went to Hugh's apartment. I had to find a list of friends to invite to the wedding. But now there isn't going to be a wedding. He was in bed with some bimbo. That's bad enough but you should have heard what he had to say. It was as if he had caught me betraying him! How could I have been so stupid for so long? We were engaged for six months and I didn't detect anything amiss. There must be something wrong with me."

"Don't blame yourself for something over which you had no control."

"But I'm usually so good at detecting phonies!"

Sargent Ramirez cleared her throat and reluctantly made her contribution. "You wouldn't be the first woman who was fooled. Some men are just no good. And we fall for them. We see in them something that nobody else sees. But sometimes it's just a mirage. You're lucky to have found out before it was too late."

❧   ❧   ❧

After a few weeks, Paul thought he should explain to Jenny what he felt for her. After all, was his quandary all that unique? He seemed to remember having read so many years before—must have been in the Songs of Songs in the Old Testament—"Thou hast ravished my heart, my sister, my bride." Isn't it then true that human experience and sentiment repeat themselves through the years, through the centuries? Was that a reflection of his very present case? Paul ended up laughing. He was taking himself entirely too seriously. His problem was to a large extent not real. After all, Paul and Jenny were not really brother and sister. That was probably true as well in the Songs of Songs—"sister" may have simply indicated a kindred soul. Surely, Jenny would realize this.

After one of their lunch meetings, he waited until the two of them were alone, if you can ever be alone in a large city.

"Jenny, I have to tell you something. I love you."

"What are you talking about? I love you too."

"What I mean is that I have fallen in love with you."

"Are you joking?"

"No, I'm in earnest."

There was a long silence. He couldn't fathom her expression. Finally she spoke.

"That's absolute nonsense. I can't accept that."

More silence followed. Her expression was cold and unresponsive. "We'd better stop seeing each other until we can straighten this out."

Paul thought, "What is there to straighten out?"

After that he felt completely confused. Had he lost her as a friend? Could he do anything to remedy the situation?

❧   ❧   ❧

Again Paul got a call from Gross and went to the station.

This time Gross had news. "Well, he took the bait!"

"Very good."

"We are guessing it's him. How many murderers could there be in town who are looking for a hit man?"

But their wait stretched out and many days later Paul wondered whether the man had smelled a trap. He hadn't made any attempt to approach the intermediary they had set up.

In the meantime, he felt uneasy about Jenny. She hadn't made any effort to contact him. Their last meeting was beginning to acquire a feeling of finality and his uneasiness was becoming anxiety.

Jenny was scheduled to give a talk to the League of Women Voters about her agency. Paul had seen the announcement during one of his visits as a volunteer. He arrived late and saw a sea of women occupying the hall and only a few empty seats in front. Two of the women sitting there gave him a hostile look. He figured they were officials of the organization who were wondering about his presence and late arrival.

Paul patiently waited until the end of Jenny's presentation. One of the women who had been sitting in the front row took over the podium and thanked Jenny for her penetrating analysis of the mission of the agency. As Jenny was stepping down, what he'd least expected happened before his eyes. A woman, or perhaps a man dressed as a woman, had pulled out a gun and was pointing it at Jenny. Everything happened too quickly. Paul wasn't close enough for an effective action against her attacker. All he could do was to interpose himself between Jenny and the gun. Just as in war, there was no time for a conscious decision. Paul jumped in front of Jenny and turned toward the shooter. An ironic twist in his mind reminded him in that instant that not too many days before he had stated that he was willing to die for her. He felt the slug hitting him and was slammed to the ground. That wasn't a small caliber gun, he thought. He was unconscious when several shots followed. This time it was from Sargent Ramirez who had been on the sidelines. The attacker crumbled to the ground. It was just his or her luck that Ramirez was the pistol champion of the district.

❦   ❦   ❦

Paul knew he was in the hospital the very instant he slowly regained consciousness. In fact, he was in the recovery room. Two slugs had been removed, he was told later. As in his previous hospital experience, he was attached to a drip and wires. Short conscious periods alternated with light sleep. Discomfort and only a muted pain were his companions.

Not surprisingly his first visitor was Gross. For a change, he had come to inform, not interrogate. Paul, still weak and still not knowing exactly what had happened, appreciated the courtesy.

"You certainly have a way of doing the unexpected! And why in hell were you there? Although thank God you were."

Gross didn't seem to want an answer and proceeded to update him. The perp, now quite dead, was not the one they anticipated. "None of the above," was the way Gross had put it. Hopefully, it was the same villain responsible for the first attack. A large withdrawal from the man's bank preceding the appearance of the hit man strongly argued for that conclusion. He had no idea what his motivation was or why he decided not to complete a second arrangement with a hit man.

"So, who was it? Are you going to keep it a secret?"

"That would be hard. It's been in the news for a while. It's George Lawrence, Edwin Lawrence's nephew. Apparently he's had an intense dislike for Ms. Lawrence for years. On top of it, he'd been found out for defrauding Mr. Lawrence's company where he worked. I understand Mr. Lawrence was not very kind to him when the theft was discovered, as you might expect. For some reason he blamed Ms. Lawrence for having been disgraced!"

Not long after Gross's official visit, Paul's parents and sister followed. Sophia was the one who expressed their dismay.

"Who would have expected something like that to happen? When you were at war we were terrified that something might happen. And it did. But this was totally unexpected. Somehow one can never relax!"

To his relief, they didn't mention that none of this would have happened if he hadn't contacted the Lawrences.

Ed and Martha Lawrence came in while the Robinsons were still there. The clumsiness of the situation was palpable but didn't last. Ed didn't skirt the issue.

"We are so sorry this happened. And of course we are grateful that you were able to defend Jenny … We'll always be immensely grateful. It was a very brave thing to do."

The absence of Jenny was so obvious that it hurt him deeply. She really didn't care for him at all, not even as a friend.

After visiting hours, she did knock shyly.

"May I come in?"

"Oh, God, of course."

"I was allowed in claiming that I was your wife! Hope you don't mind," She said with a hint of a smile as she sat on the side of the bed. "To tell the truth I am ashamed and embarrassed. You saved my life twice and I have been avoiding you. When this happened, I was told you were in the hospital and I thought I'd better have something meaningful to say before coming. I've been so confused!"

"Wherever I am, you'll always be welcome. You don't have to explain anything. You don't owe me anything, not gratitude or pity. I did what was in me."

"Well, there is a lot to explain. Everything was sudden and unexpected. Hugh's behavior. Two attempts on my life. Two dead men. A betrayal from a close relative. I have to confess that I am totally confused. I do love you. Whether it can become romantic love, I don't know. Let's be friends for now. Good friends. I can't think of anybody I feel closer to."

"Thank you for coming and explaining. I'm sure it was hard. For now I'll settle for that!"

Nevertheless he felt a warm glow which he knew would never fade. They stayed holding hands for a long time.

THE END OF THE GAME

Mark Markowitz pushed himself up from the bed to reach the wheelchair. With more effort he was able to turn himself and sit on it. His shoulders and the joints in his arms ached but the effort allowed him to regain some dignity. Dignity! If you could call it that. Perhaps an ounce of self-respect. The physical and mental contortions he had to put himself through just because the powers that be had announced a visitor! Receiving a visitor from his bed was to him distasteful and that is why he felt he had to go through all those contortions to reach his chair. When his strands of gray hair were combed back and he had bothered shaving, as he had on this occasion, he knew that he looked present- able but that didn't help.

He never had any visitors apart from his sour middle-aged daughter, once a year just before the holidays. But they had nothing to talk about. She did not respect him and he thought that without that any real communication was impossible. This caller was a total mystery, possibly giving the visit some piquancy. Ann Marrine. He didn't even remember that name.

The woman who entered with a smile was of an age he hadn't expected. Per- haps she was in her twenties, although he knew his judgement of age had become suspect, like so many of his critical judgements. He hadn't seen a young person since he had found himself in these premises, five years before. He looked at her with incipient grouchiness. That was his standard way of greeting anybody. This new visitor must be a new ploy, one those damn social workers with their ersatz cheerfulness and useless counselling. But she didn't follow the pattern. For one thing she greeted him as Mr. Markowitz, instead of the usual discourteous and presumptuous "Mark." The smile seemed to be spontaneous, if that were possible. She extended her hand, and automatically he shook it.

"I'm Anne Marrine."

"I don't know you—never heard your name!"

Her new amused smile was disconcerting. "I don't see how you could have heard it before. My grandmother was Evelyn McPherson, neé Paulson; if you search the corners of your mind, you might remember her. She died last week."

If she expected condolences, she could wait forever. "I don't know her."

"She made me promise to talk to you. How are you Mr. Markowitz?"

"Waiting to die, of course. Can't be much fun."

The amused smile reappeared. "You must know best. Some people find life not much fun."

"Why are you here?"

"Well let me tell you a story my grandmother told me just before she died." Markowitz cleared his throat and Ann Marrine continued, "You were the big cheese of Continent Unlimited. That you must recall."

"Continent Unlimited—a bunch of stiff-necked bastards."

"I see you recall that well enough!" And she started with her tale.

Evelyn Paulson stood in front of Mr. Markowitz, the boss of bosses. A man was sitting next to them taking notes. She wasn't crying, although tears were crowding her eyes, blurring her vision. She did her best to suppress a sob. Although overcome by desperation, she didn't want to elicit pity or sympathy. That was not her way. Too proud, probably, her main fault. She was only too conscious of her appearance. Eyes swollen from crying. A red face bloated by despair. Dirty matted blonde hair. A mess.

"You absconded with $300 and you admit that." To my surprise, Markowitz thought. "And all you can say is that you had been desperate."

"I thought I could return at least part of the money before I got caught."

"Why were you 'desperate'?" The query was overlaid with sarcasm.

She was stumbling on the words. "My mom … my mom … is in the hospital … and I have … have to feed two little ones."

Markowitz turned to the man next to him. "Marlowe, go find out whether it's true." After the man left, Markowitz got up and addressed Evelyn Paulson again. "I have to leave for a while. You can wait here until I come back."

They had devised a new way of torturing her. It all seemed a way to punish her further as her anxiety escalated. What on earth was in their minds? The temptation of standing up and leaving was strong. She was to be fired, she was sure. Probably the police would be called in and that almost certainly would mean some time in jail. She just wished they'd give her the time to find a babysitter willing to stay for a long period with her little siblings. But what would she have to pay her with? Mrs. Merlaine who was now with the kids could be counted on only for afternoons or perhaps a full day at a time. Evelyn recognized how desperate her situation was.

It took forever for Markowitz to reappear. Evelyn could smell the pastry he must have been chewing on.

"Have you ever been in trouble before?"

Evelyn was amused, despite everything. What on earth was happening? "In high school. I made the mistake of answering back when admonished and eventually my mom took me out of the school."

She was surprised at the twitch on Mr. Markowitz's lips. It might have been a smile.

"These are the conditions I wish to offer you. You get transferred to a section where you won't handle cash. You'll be paid the same. You are given $500 as a loan. It will come out of your pay, $10 at a time. You immediately return the $300, so that no crime has been committed."

Evelyn didn't know why, after all her effort to appear calm, she suddenly couldn't contain herself and broke into tears. She felt his hand patting her in the back. "Good luck, and I hope I won't see you again, unless it's in line with our work." And he was gone.

❧   ❧   ❧

"Grandma thought you'd saved her life. She went on with her life—had children—a grand child, namely me. She wanted me to say thank you. She had never got around to that. You certainly remember the incident, don't you?"

Markowitz had no recollection of the episode at all, but the girl seemed to be so enthusiastic he suddenly felt he couldn't deny her. "I certainly do. It was a high moment in my life." Besides, he thought, it feels good not to have been a bastard all of your life and perhaps Ann would come visiting again. He liked her smile. It was well worth having combed his hair and shaved for the occasion.

THE RAIN

The rain was unremitting—most of the time just a drizzle, at times as if it was gushing from the sky. Police Chief Margen had a good view of the day's grayness from the window of his office. A parking lot drenched to a shiny black—the trees lining its edge agitated by the wind. The woman sobbing on the bench on the hall next to the door only contributed to the cheerless atmosphere of the day. His mood as usual was also somber.

In a small town with a small police force, just five men, the chief always had to be involved in the violent tragedies as well as everyday minutiae. From the report due yesterday, to the rare murder or larceny to Mrs. Strossberg's cat up a tree. This time he felt personally involved. He had noticed the woman, identified after the accident as Florence Interman, sitting alone at the diner's table. Short dark hair, young and pretty, if it weren't for her vacant look and blank face, as if she was in shock, as if something terrible had happened to her. Margen felt that she looked vaguely familiar—perhaps a face from his past. He should have talked to her then, but he held back only to meet her later at the site of a crash.

The car she had sideswiped had turned over. The site was at a curve on a God-forsaken part of the highway. Past the shoulder of the road, water-drenched grasses and a few forlorn bushes, the upturned car looked like an overturned giant beetle, burning. Joe Miller and Phil Swift in their blue and gold cruiser had reached the scene first. Before the car was engulfed in flames, they had pulled out two people, a child of perhaps two and her mother. The acrid smell of the fire was in the air as the ambulance took them away, sirens screaming. Ms. Interman sat in her car, its front end mashed in. Physically, she hadn't suffered much. The safety belt and the discharged air bag had fulfilled their function. She'd refused medical care. Her wounds were in her soul. She kept murmuring, "The poor child … the poor child."

Margen talked her into accompanying him to the police station. Haste was advisable. Any minute, the gas tank of the wreck might explode. At a distance, the wail of the fire engine taking over from the ambulance screams which had faded away. There was no way of turning her loose into the world. Her testimony had been monosyllabic. "Yes," to the question of whether she had been at fault in misjudging distances. "No," she hadn't been drinking, a declaration quickly confirmed by a breathalyser. There was no way of turning her loose into the world. She was functioning only minimally.

The wallet in her purse revealed the name of her husband, and the person to notify in case of an emergency, Bob Interman. The number was local. The phone rang a few times before being picked up. Margen identified himself and explained.

"There is no point in me coming. We are estranged," Interman said and then hung up.

Margen was not easily discouraged. He rang again. "It's Chief Margen again. She needs you. If you're not here within twenty minutes, I'll send a squad car for you, and if you are not at your house, I'll start an all points alert." The legal niceties could be left for later.

Interman came and was brought in by the only woman detective on the force, Alice Wohmann, who following instructions had been waiting for him in the front. He was a rather good-looking man with regular features, dark hair, and under his black raincoat, shorts and t-shirt. He looked peeved and indignant.

"I told you that I can't contribute anything."

"Nice of you to come, Mr. Interman. Your wife is in some kind of a shock. You should take her to the hospital and have her checked out. For now I want you to be here for her. You can start with a hug. She needs one." He thought, 'You fucked up somehow. Now it's your job to help.' Margen had been struck many a time by the therapeutic effect of hugs—best if heartfelt, but always effective.

Interman was reluctant and had an unpleasant expression on his face but the cold imperious look from Margen didn't leave him much choice. He sat next to Florence and put one arm around her and then the other. She melted into his arms and murmured, "Thank you, Bob … Thank you. I'm glad I can still count on you."

Interman seemed mollified by her response and her obvious need and tightened his embrace.

Alice Wohmann brought them coffee, a role she would have rejected under ordinary circumstances. After sitting for a few minutes, Florence was talked into seeking medical attention. Margen followed husband and wife to the hospital in his car intent on getting first hand news about the two accident victims.

At the glass door, which he reached just before the Intermans, he noticed a man in a rain coat, waiting, his right hand in his pocket. Margen's sixth sense screamed a silent warning. He grabbed the hand as it was leaving the stranger's pocket and clamped down on the fingers holding the gun. Staying to the side with his quarry, he let the Intermans enter and then removed the gun from the man's grasp. Without a word handcuffs were quickly placed on the stranger's wrists. The man didn't protest. Margen pulled him into his car. "Let me see your wallet," he ordered.

He took out the driver's license from the man's wallet, which identified him as Steven Mathews.

"So what's going on?" he asked.

Mathews was now sobbing. "She killed my wife! She killed my little girl!"

"Does that give you a license to murder?"

"She killed them! She killed them!"

Margen pulled out a cellular phone and punched in a number.

"This is Chief Margen. Could you tell me the condition of the Mathews baby and her mother?"

He waited a while. "Christ! I knew it would be easier if I stopped by. Find the doctor and ask."

He waited a while, and after listening, "Don't give me that confidentiality shit, this is a police matter. You can give some hints if nothing else." After listening, he then turned to Mathews. "Listen, little asshole. They are both doing fairly well. The little girl is okay. Her mother broke a leg. Okay?" He then continued. "Attempted murder would get you a few years, maybe ten or fifteen. Carrying an unlicenced weapon might get just five. What shall it be?"

"I was just trying to scare her!"

"Bullshit! How would it feel not to see you wife and little girl for a few years, except through bars?"

Mathews was now crying silently.

"If you ever get the chance again, think before acting like a moron. Suppose they were dead, what good would it do to murder the poor woman?"

"I told you, I wasn't going to kill her."

"I think for the moment we will slam you in jail for disorderly conduct. I'll think about what to do later."

Margen thought a weapons charge would be unavoidable. The DA would have the final word. Unfortunately, the woman and baby might need him, although Margen couldn't see how such a fool would be much help in the long run.

There was plenty of paperwork to clear up at his desk, but Margen felt alone with his own personal troubles.

He got on his phone again.

"Sorry Marge. I got stuck again."

"Two disappointed boys don't mean anything to you. Not to mention the arrangements I had to make. Once a jerk, always a jerk!"

"You're right, but can we talk?"

"What would that accomplish? You can't even keep your word."

"Marge, I promise it will important for the boys. How about tomorrow at 9 am?"

"Forget it. There are a number of things I have to do and if you plan to come you'll disappoint the boys again."

"Please Marge. Give me a time."

"Make it 12 noon. If you're not here then, I will never talk to you again. If you call on the phone, I'll hang up."

He thought, 'that sounds familiar' and then he said. "Okay Marge, 12 noon."

The trip took the usual sixty minutes. With great trepidation, he rang the bell of the familiar house. Marge opened the door and cast him a sour look. Still very attractive despite her antagonism, he felt a tug at his heart. She spoke first without a greeting.

"Well, you made it for a change."

She must have sent the boys away expecting fireworks. He didn't hear the usual pattern of little feet when they came to meet him. Something hit him then—so many lost opportunities!

"Marge, let's sit down for a minute." She let him in with a mock gesture of welcome and the two of them sat separated by a few feet on the familiar couch in the room he had known so well.

He let silence prevail, then he spoke softly. "Please listen. You can yell at me afterwards if you think it's deserved. I know you've dedicated your life to the boys. That's fine. But I'd like to look to their future. Regardless of your dedication, I think they need me. I mean they need me more than once a week or thereabouts. I can never match my present salary if I move again to be close to them. Perhaps we could try to make ends meet. Perhaps I can save some money for the next few months before moving. But my monthly pay-ments—alimony and the kids' support—may be at risk. If you're willing to take a chance, I feel it's worth the try."

"Sure, that's easy for you to say. The real gamble would be mine. Besides, you'd always be in my hair."

"I promise that I'll leave your private life alone. But yes, there is a big risk. Too bad I can't transfer my job. It isn't as demanding as the one I had before. After all, I'm the boss and every so often I can skip the long hours. Last night was an exceptional case. A woman seemed to be wiped out, dysfunctional. Such a young kid! I think she had a serious quarrel with her husband. I couldn't leave her alone; I don't think she would have survived."

"Is that it? A woman you don't even know is more important than your children?"

"Marge, it wasn't a trivial matter, I think the woman's whole existence was at stake. I must confess that there is another factor I didn't realize at the time. She resembles the little girl who turned my life around. I never told you the details. As you know in school I was a disciplinary problem. In middle school, along with others I harassed girls in my class. Once I locked myself in a store room with Lillian Smith. She was a cute little thing with bobbed dark hair and big blue eyes. I just wanted to scare her although it probably would have gotten me to reform school or perhaps beyond. It might have counted as sexual assault if she had said so to get even. Lillian was not scared at all. Perhaps not exactly in these words she asked me, "Where will this get you? You don't like doing what you're told to do. If you continue this way you will have to do what people tell you for the rest of your life." I might have sneered at that. Soon, there was an insistent knocking and the voice of the assistant principal. I was really scared. Lillian made me hide in the closet and pretended to have been locked in from the outside. I didn't realize how much I owed her until later. We were in the same class. I hadn't even known she had observed my wretched behavior."

"Oh! How romantic! Your absence went back to your experience in middle school." Her voice was dripping with sarcasm. "At one time you had a much better imagination."

Some malfunctions can never be remedied, he felt as he left.

In his office later in the afternoon, he realized he had been sufficiently upset to forget to eat. He wasn't hungry but he knew that he might have a long vigil later. He called a pizza and sub place. The desk clerk and dispatcher, Bernice, buzzed him when the food arrived.

He had a terrible night and was sure that more would come in the future. Groggy from lack of sleep he tried to revive himself with a cup of strong coffee. Hopping into his car, he stopped at Miss Thompson's bakery. He reached his office at his usual time, chewing on a pastry. A few minutes later, he had just had time to start looking at the papers on his desk when Bernice rang him on the phone. "You have a call."

"Well, put it through." He didn't understand the reluctance in her voice.

"It's your wife." He realized then that his associates knew more about his personal life than he had realized. He might as well face the stark facts now, Marge must have found a way of blasting at him again.

"Marge," he said.

There was a long silence at the other end, and then, "I thought about it a lot … I know you love those boys and I know they need you. Perhaps we can move where you are now. There isn't much that holds us here and I understand the schools are good where you are. We'll have to work out the details very carefully. I don't want you around messing up my life, but you can certainly see the boys as often as you want. And I sure hope you'll do that."

Margen gulped trying to find the right words. He felt unexpected tears reaching his eyes. All he could mumble was, "Thank you, thank you."

Looking out of the window, Margen saw that the rain had finally stopped. Although the sun hadn't come out yet, the bright sky held a promise of better times.

THREE-CARD MONTE

In this age of mangled names and words—nicknames, abbreviations, anagrams, a few letters stuck together, Louis Brockard went by the name "Brock." Brock had been drawn to the wedding of Beth, an old girlfriend. Or if you want to be precise, the girl who'd ditched him in no uncertain words. Thinking about it, Brock realized that even with the regret and pain, the parting had been the way he preferred. No false statements, promises, wails, excuses. She didn't think they had much in common. Perhaps what she said was the true reason. Perhaps, she just didn't cotton to him after the first few blissful weeks. When it had happened, he was hurt but he had always suspected he wasn't in the same class as Beth. The proof is in the pudding: she was about to marry the ideal bachelor in a mansion in the middle of a park rented for the occasion. The groom, Ethan Monshire, had money, tradition, education and good manners. In contrast, Brock never knew exactly what he was wearing or what he should be wearing and frequently couldn't put two words together to save his soul. He wasn't stupid, but had he tried couldn't have completed the *New York Times* crossword puzzle either.

Brock had made sure that he wouldn't meet Beth again. Perhaps he still had strong feelings for her; he wasn't a masochist. Pain wasn't one of his objectives. He even refused to talk to her on the phone. Breakups had to be final. It made no sense to be hurt twice. Then, why was he at her wedding? He had no idea. It was a contradiction to his avoidance strategy. Perhaps it was an attempt to bring closure to a painful episode in his life.

Beth, in traditional wedding dress, was brought in on the arm of her boss, a renown and successful attorney. Always pretty, she was more so in white, with black hair setting off her smooth lovely clear skin. The bride had come forward before the groom had arrived and without the traditional wedding march, possibly to quiet the twenty or so people present who were becoming restive.

Brock remembered that she really didn't have much of a family. There were no siblings and her mother would have objected if Beth had invited her father. It had been a bitter divorce. Mother was sitting in front, in tears. Grandma was sitting next to her—a woman with incongruously loose long gray hair and young mischievous green eyes. Brock had met them both and was enchanted by Grandma who in her youth had been part of a magician's act—what today is called an illusionist. She still knew how to charm. Beth had told him many stories about her grandmother. How she could make things disappear and reappear. How a bush would produce silver dollars. How with playing cards the one you just selected with your thoughts would edge out of the card deck she held.

They waited and waited for the groom, Brock in the periphery, hoping that Beth wouldn't notice him. There was a continual buzz from the puzzled group. Somebody ran to the best man and whispered in his ear. Beth broke into tears even before the announcement was made that Ethan would not be coming. Brock was much disturbed—certainly, Beth didn't deserve the public humiliation. He left. This time the pain wasn't his; he felt sympathy for the poor girl.

He was walking to his car when Beth in her bridal dress with a trailing veil came running and grabbed him by the arm.

"Take me out of here, Brock. Please!" And then she was sobbing uncontrollably. The whole world had gone topsy-turvy. Brock was totally confused. Had she recognized him from behind? Had he been selected as a friend or was he the first person she'd found whom she knew? He followed his instincts and opened the passenger door. He made sure she was sitting with her gown and train tucked in against her, and then after closing the door, sitting in the driver's seat he started the motor.

"Listen Beth! I'll take you out of here, to any place you want but wouldn't you do better with a girlfriend? Your mother? A relative?"

"Let's just get out of here!"

With the car in motion he asked, "Where to?"

"Any place. I don't want to see anybody I know." And then after a pause, "We were supposed to leave for Hawaii tomorrow morning." And then silence.

"Okay. I'll take you to my place. You can stay there or go to a hotel. But the wedding dress won't do."

"Shit!"

"Where's your stuff?"

"At Penny's. We were to take off right away. It's all packed. But I can't go there." Penny had shared an apartment with her until Beth had moved in with Ethan.

"That's exactly where we are going to go. I can park around the corner and you can stay in the car. We might have to wait for Penny. I imagine she must have been with the rest of the crowd."

It was not a long wait. At the door of the apartment, Penny sneered at him. "What are you doing here? Ready to gloat?"

Brock didn't think her remark deserved an answer. "She's with me. She asked me to pick up her suitcase."

Penny's stare didn't soften but she did direct him to the suitcase.

For Brock the situation was awkward to say the least. In his apartment, scared by Beth's crying jag, he held her in a hug. He knew it was required—the need of one human being for another. The hug, the sympathy, had nothing to do with their love life.

It took a long time after she calmed down for him to ask her a question. "What about your dad? Is something wrong with him?"

"What do you mean?"

"He lives on the West Coast. If you get along with him perhaps you could have a change of scenery and start anew."

"There is nothing wrong with him. But if I call him Mother would never forgive me! Besides, I haven't seen him for five years. I can stay here. What are you bitching about? You were always ready to hop in bed with me."

"Beth, when I was in love it was different. Now it would be a mistake."

"Phooey! You are totally incapable of falling in love. You don't want me now because somebody else has discarded me."

Brock was surprised by her tone and her lack of insight.

"Look, you couldn't have had a worse shock. You need time to get over it. You can stay here as long as you want. Eventually you would be better in a hotel, or going back to Penny's, or I'll help you find a new place."

Without saying anything, she just looked at him, her blue eyes brimming with tears.

Brock had no idea how the notion had taken hold and germinated. After a few hours Beth had calmed down and exclaimed, "Here, for the first time in my life I have a chance to travel with first class tickets and first rate hotels all over the world and it's all going to waste."

Why something so mundane had appeared in her mind, he couldn't tell. However, something was cooking in her head, he could tell. Regret? Pain? Or something else entirely? He couldn't understand how she could have gone from despair to such strange reflections. He thought he had to break the mood."Let's go see a movie. You need the distraction. And maybe I do too."

They did go to a movie. Beth seemed to have found her composure and neither one of them really watched the movie. In the semi-darkness, Brock suddenly noted how lovely she really was and felt an unwelcome stirring. Finally, after they went for coffee her hints were put into words. "Why don't we, you and I, use the reservations that were meant for the honeymoon?"

"Beth! That's crazy. I imagine most of the reservations can be canceled, maybe with a penalty but that would be the most rationale thing. Why would you want to be with me? It seems to me it's your way of getting even with Ethan or the whole unkind world!"

Beth ignored the tenor of his protest. "I just don't want to lose the opportunity. Look it's all paid for. When was the last time you were in Hawaii, India, Singapore, China?"

"Beth! That's still crazy. I have a job, the two of us haven't seen each other for months. We broke up a long time ago. It doesn't make any sense." He wondered how she could have gotten over her desertion so quickly or perhaps the trauma had affected her good sense.

But she continued, "I'm sure they'll give you time off for your honeymoon! Perhaps not for a near fatal illness, but they would for a honeymoon! It would be un-American not to! All it would take is a few white lies and switching names on the reservations. I imagine you have a passport! These days you can't even come back from Canada without a passport!"

"Yes, shit! I have a passport from when I was planning to go to France."

"So, there! Another argument in favor of what I want to do. You never even went to France. Your plans fell through! This is one time when they won't."

Brock regretted almost immediately having consented to accompany her on their bizarre trip. But then why should it matter? He might be helping her get through a rough patch. He rejected the idea that she still cared for him.

Side by side on the airplane that would carry them to a different world, he felt a strong sense of comradery as if they were about to embark on a great adventure together. They spoke to each other as if they had been good friends for a long time—with no surprises and an unexpected degree of intimacy.

The first night at a hotel on their supposed honeymoon, he felt very uncomfortable sharing the room with Beth. He had no clues about how she might feel. Her attitude although friendly was detached. Since there was another bed that could be pulled out of the couch, there was no need to share her bed, although the thought had occurred to him.

Much later on, when in their first day in Hawaii, the sun was setting over the blue sea in all its splendor. On the promenade, he didn't know what had taken hold of him. Beth had smiled at him—a pleased, affectionate smile. After having built all those formidable defenses, he found himself embracing her and kissing her passionately and even more surprising she responded. It didn't take them long to return to the hotel overwhelmed by desire and passion. Brock had no understanding of what was happening. He had never experienced anything so overwhelming. More surprising, Beth must have felt the same way. How they had turned their travel into a true honeymoon was a mystery. All he knew for sure was that he loved her and that it was reciprocated.

The morning after a night of passion gave him a chance to reflect. Beth was stirring next to him. She slid toward him and put her arms around him.

"Beth, there is something you didn't tell me.'Fess up. What's happening?"

There was a long silence in which she avoided his eyes, but then she spoke. "Please don't hate me for it and I'll promise I'll never manipulate you again."

"So, what happened?"

"Ethan and I broke up a week before the scheduled wedding. It was a mismatch and we both realized it. In my case I realized I was in love with you despite everything. I also realized that you were foolish enough not to want to talk to me for whatever reason."

Beth was terrified about Brock's possible response and hesitated. Brock nudged: "Yes?"

She found the courage to continue. There was no way she could hide the truth, "Grandma, who was paying for the wedding and honeymoon, talked me into not canceling the arrangements. She had seen through me all along and knew what I felt for you. Her instincts told her that you loved me still. She said that it would be like three-card monte. You can't guess which card is the right one and that's when the illusionist comes in. I'm sorry, I really shouldn't have done it. If you want to cancel the rest of the trip, let us do it now."

"So all that crying was a fake."

"I don't know. I didn't force it. The unexpected humiliation was real and I was sure that the ploy wouldn't work and I was going to lose you for good."

"Do you really love me or are you making another mistake?"

"Please don't be mean."

"Would you marry me if I asked?"

"Are you teasing me?"

Brock shook his head. "If we got married right now, it would be a real honeymoon."

"Sounds just right. Hurray for tradition! But now I'm starved. Let's go to breakfast. Later, we can seal our union again. I think that a marriage ceremony can be arranged here just as well as in the continental USA."

THE INTERVIEW

The question had been unexpected. Marie Robertson closed her eyes for an instant and opened them immediately knowing that her face would appear on television as emphasized by the presence of various cameras. The hotel lobby was flooded with lights and several eager faces of reporters were lifted anticipating an interesting answer by the woman contesting a powerful political machine for a seat in Congress.

"Isn't it true that an interview with your husband was held back because it's too nasty? It's no secret that the two of you don't get along."

As upset as she was her self-defense mechanism came to the surface, thank God! "I had nothing to do with that. You'll have to ask my husband."

What had he done now? Had she hurt him that much? Was he that vindictive?

"Please ask me questions about my programs and plans for the future. What I would do as a Congressperson. Isn't that what your listeners are really interested in?"

The questioner, a glamorous blonde woman in her prime, gave her a photogenic smile. "Certainly. But aren't ethical considerations part of the job?"

That wasn't too difficult to answer. "Certainly. I hope Mr. Powerly's ethics will also be considered." It was rumored that her opponent, Eugene Powerly, was about to be indicted for taking bribes. Not that it would make much of a difference. He was a very popular man, with a great smile and a glib tongue. His constituency was very forgiving.

Later in her hotel room Marie covered her eyes moist with tears. The whole campaign had evolved into a one-sided, snide spreading of rumors. It was a disaster. Questions about her marriage had been raised. A rumor had spread that she hadn't taken proper care of her children. Much had been made about the death by anaphylactic shock of her step-daughter so many years before.

What made it much harder was that she felt guilty about it. She had been a nurse before her marriage, a time she regarded with nostalgia. Her inability to do anything useful for her daughter still haunted her. Diphenylhydramine and aminophylline hadn't done any good. It had been a terrible episode in their lives.

Just few minutes before leaving her hotel room for the evening, her experienced campaign manager, Carlos Mossek, had shaken his head sorrowfully. The polls had been very negative. She should withdraw if she couldn't take the heat.

There were two arguments against a withdrawal. She would appear to be admitting the truthfulness of the charges, and she would feel like a coward the rest of her life. The fact that the opposition was using such dirty tactics was clearly an indication that they were not only tainted but also scared that she might win.

The telephone rang. The metallic unfriendly voice of Mirta Voll emanated. Marie cringed—wished she hadn't picked it up. The hotel desk wasn't supposed to put any calls through except if it was from one of her two daughters.

"Marie, I just played Bob's interview. You must have heard about it. I think you should listen to it even at this late hour."

Oh, God! Marie knew that it would tear her apart. That might well be Mirta's intention. They had competed for jobs and Marie had found Mirta merciless and nasty. Now Mirta was a big wheel in RBC. She headed the news programs. Yes, perhaps she should listen to the recording, although it might devastate her. Twenty-five years of marriage seemed to have melted into altercations and antagonism. She could let Carlos listen to it. But no. It was her job and besides she might not want to share its contents. It was bad enough that Mirta had listened to it. She hoped that the decision not to air it would not be reversed.

God knows what had happened to their marriage. They seemed to have lost the capacity to talk to each other meaningfully. They had had a public altercation in a restaurant. How foolish of her. But she couldn't let it go by. She had developed a crush for one of the men in her political entourage. But that had been over. Besides nothing had happened. She was sure Bob thought she had slept with the man but that hadn't happened, although she didn't know why not. It was probably because she was so old-fashioned! The warmth had gone out of their marriage. Bob had said the nastiest things. Now he had the opportunity to put them on the public record.

"Very thoughtful of you, Mirta." When necessary, she could pour out hypocrisy like anybody else in public life. "When could we get together?"

"Why not right now? I think it would make a difference in your campaign."

Sure, Mirta was enjoying her poison. "Can I just come over?"

"If you're not too tired."

"I am, but you make it sound like an emergency."

"Far from it. But if I were you I wouldn't wait."

Marie had to sign a book at the front desk and show some ID before being allowed in. The modern building, all marble and glass, seemed to be mostly empty at that late hour, although she could hear some subdued sounds of activity. She was escorted to Ms. Voll's office. Surprisingly for such a high-ranking position, Mirta was still at work. Perhaps even more surprising was she hadn't kept Marie waiting. Mirta smiled at her, her usual photogenic and meaningless smile. She got up from her desk.

"Come on in. Come on in. I have the VCR ready. Please close the door. It's really very interesting."

They both sat on comfortable chairs in front of the set. Marie's mouth was dry and she folded her hands together to hide their tremor.

Mirta explained, "We recorded it because Bob could only come at a very bad time. Then, I thought I would hold it back until you'd had a chance to watch it."

The interview started in the usual way. Handsome George Napolitano shook Bob's hand. Bob appeared calm and pleasant. Marie hadn't seen him like that in years.

"We are so glad that you were able to come. With such a contentious political campaign we thought you could throw light on one of the candidates, namely your wife."

"I'm glad to be here and to be able to set the record straight. Thank you for inviting me."

"I understand you're in the middle of divorce proceedings."

Bob smiled. He seemed to want to match the interviewer smile for smile—charm for charm.

"That is not correct. We have had our differences. I might say that all marriages have ups and downs. At the moment we are in a down phase. And that's all you or the public are entitled to know. Let me tell you about her character and her abilities to serve as a congresswoman."

Marie swallowed hard. "Here it comes," she thought.

"Marie is a most unusual woman. I was lucky to have found and married her. She is thoroughly dedicated to public service. She is strong, bright and will face all issues calmly and impartially. Her ethics are of the highest. The district couldn't do any better."

"There have been rumors about the way she raised her children."

Bob laughed an amused laugh. "All you have to do is look at the results. Amanda is a senior at Brandeis and Rose has a fellowship to start MIT this fall. Two very bright, well-adjusted women each with a terrific sense of humor." Bob turned suddenly very serious. "I suppose you are referring to the vicious rumors about what happened to Louisa. The poor girl died. I was there. I called the hospital for an ambulance; these were the days before 911. Marie, who had been a nurse, did everything that could be done. I think Mr. Powerly should dissociate himself from those nasty rumors and perhaps even apologize if anybody in his campaign was involved."

Marie hardly listened to the rest. When Napolitano asked Bob how the two of them had met, Mirta turned off the set. "We'll show part of it tomorrow evening. The rest is just routine. I thought you might want to hear what he had to say and take advantage."

Marie was deeply moved by what Bob had said and Mirta's attitude. She felt her eyes well up with tears.

"Thank you, Mirta. I needed that."

Back in the hotel she called Bob. She probably had woken him up.

"Bob! I'm sorry if I woke you up."

"I haven't been sleeping all that well."

"I want to thank you for that interview."

"I didn't say anything that wasn't true."

"I'm glad to see we are still friends. Could we get together to talk?"

"Whenever you're free."

She felt that was one night when both of them could sleep.

KEVIN CARWELL

Kevin had just returned to civilization, if you could call Bergentown that—a collection of corrals and barns along with a hotel, a church and at least two saloons and one brothel. Tired and dirty, his clothes were torn and stiff from caked dirt and dried blood. It was lucky that he had a few silver dollars left. His Stetson marked by sweat and dirt, he kept. But he replaced the rest of his clothes with new purchases in the dry goods store where Charlie Benjamin reigned. The shopkeeper had a bulbous nose, a small gray mustache accompanied by a ruddy complexion and a large mole on one cheek. He had been gossiping with two elderly creatures.

"Got into some trouble, didn'tcha?"

Kevin didn't think the comment needed an answer. He had known Charlie for some time but didn't enjoy his conversations. After a welcome bath and shave in the rooming house, he had decided that he deserved a stiff drink.

In the saloon he nursed the bourbon, his first in months. A stranger, very big and muscular with a small gray mustache, approached his table. He had an unwashed appearance and discolored teeth. Some hair strands, black and gray, peeked from under his cowboy hat. A pitted red nose stood on a face covered with sparse short black and gray hairs. He hunkered down at the table in front of Kevin and asked, "Kevin Carwell?" Kevin nodded. "If you know what's good for you, you'll come with me." The gun the man suddenly produced and held under the table, a Colt six-shooter, was more eloquent. And that was the beginning of Kevin's new odyssey.

"Vamoos," the man said and Kevin didn't have much choice. It had been a mistake to return to town. Although there was nothing to hold him, everybody knew who he was and he had just reported to the sheriff what had happened up at Upper Gulch Pass.

Kevin sensed that this was a new episode in a tortuous saga he'd thought had reached its end. Kevin and three other men had been deputized to find the lost money and the U.S. mail. The stagecoach had been expected in town early in the afternoon. But during an armed robbery interrupted by gun fire, the coach had tumbled down a ravine while trying to avoid its fate. Both bandit and escort riding shotgun had been killed in the exchange. The driver and two passengers, one in bandages, had arrived on foot two days later with the sad story.

Kevin and his three companions had pinpointed the location of the coach. There was no way of getting down to where it had fallen without ropes and some expertise. For that they would have to return to town. An argument over how to proceed, whether to return to town without revealing their finding with the intention of keeping the loot, or to get help so that the money and mail could be recovered, terminated when Kevin was overruled by two bullets.

Death had taunted him, but he had survived. The scars still looked and felt raw. After being shot he had fallen down an embankment. He had survived and had been able to crawl to where there were deep wagon tracks. A family on a wagon on their way to settle wherever chance might take them and looking for a place to camp had found him. They provided him with the essentials—food, water and improvised clean bandages. His rescuers had left him at the Dew Drop Ranch where he was sheltered until his recovery. Fortunately, the Carwells always had had strong constitutions. Until he was hung supposedly for cattle rustling, Carwell's father had survived many bloody encounters with bad men as well as the law.

Bent on evening the score, Kevin, rifle and handgun on the ready, had searched for his errant companions. Unfortunately all he had found were their remains. Matt, his only friend among the lot, Kevin had recognized with a pang. Sobbing uncontrollably he had buried them using a shovel that had been left behind. There had been a measure of relief among the pain. Even if they had turned on him, dealing severely with friends or acquaintances would have been an unwelcome task. Obviously, their attackers must have been after the money.

Kevin concluded that the money hadn't been recovered. Facing the stranger, he swallowed hard. He was tired and distraught and might not be able to face the new challenge. They walked out of the saloon. If the gun at Kevin's back had attracted any attention, nobody had dared interfere. After relieving Kevin of his gun, the man made it clear that he wanted to be led to the stagecoach and its treasure.

Kevin thought he probably was one of the men who had killed his companions.

They were soon on their way. A young girl, Agnes, probably still in her teens, along with the three horses they were riding and two more accompanied Kevin and the man. To Kevin, the girl looked vaguely familiar. Although drab, she was not unattractive and wore a worn-out faded dress. Agnes called his captor, Bart. The two couldn't have been friends. Bart only barked orders at her and other exchanges between the two was rare. Kevin couldn't guess what held the two together.

In the evening, they prepared to camp. Bart found a spot next to a small stream. He pulled some jerky out from the saddlebags. Coffee and canned beans warmed on the fire, were their fare Agnes brought on tin plates which she later washed in the stream.

Bart expected them to sleep stretched out on the ground, and at his command, Agnes distributed several blankets. He chained the reclining Kevin to a tree and then stretched out uphill from them, with a rifle at the ready.

The gnawing fear in Kevin's stomach was hard to ignore. To calm his nerves he forced himself to concentrate on the world around him. There was no way of escaping but he found some respite in the calm surroundings. The night was clear and Kevin noted the stars above. The moon was just a sliver in the sky. The smells were of pines and grass. An owl was hooting not too far from where they lay. He had learned to ignore the drove of mosquitoes. Sometimes during the night his mind would waken to his dangers. There was little hope for him with Bart having the upper hand. Suddenly Kevin remembered the time he had seen Agnes before in a happier time.

A man had suddenly turned on the woman sitting with him in a tavern. He had slapped her hard so that she had been ejected from her chair. She was probably from the brothel next door. The few respectable women in town wouldn't be in a saloon. The violence had rubbed Kevin the wrong way and he had suddenly stood up. Before the man had been able to pull out his gun, Kevin had immobilized his wrist and hit him with his right fist. The episode was over faster than it had started. Kevin had helped the woman up and walked her to where she wanted to go. At their knock, Agnes, who must have been a servant or maid, had opened the door of the brothel.

The woman he had rescued, whose name turned out to be Rose, had pulled him inside. She had to relate the episode to her companions and a middle-aged woman dressed conservatively, the well-known Madame Bonjour. Women of different sizes and shades and varying degrees of undress had quickly congregated. Kevin had never been in a brothel, never seen female flesh exposed. To the amusement of the women, he'd been embarrassed and felt himself blushing. Besides, in her narrative, Rose had grossly exaggerated his role in the affair. Madame Bonjour offered him an unlimited sampling of their offerings and the women had burst out laughing when he'd stammered that he had to leave.

The story of what had happened had buzzed around town for a while, so much so that his adversary had judged it best to leave.

Bart and his charges broke up their bivouac early in the morning. In the confusion, Kevin was able to ask Agnes, "How did you join this horse's ass?"

"He's my uncle. Bonjour would have stopped him if she could."

Bart interrupted with a yell. "What are the two yaking about?" A fist sent Agnes sprawling on the ground. "One more word and I'll kill you!"

Kevin felt completely helpless. His hands had formed fists but he knew that his intervention would accomplish nothing. Agnes, getting up uncowed, indicated that his decision not to intervene had been the right choice. After that he felt that at least he had one friend.

Eventually, they reached their destination. Despite his anxiety, Kevin was amused. A rustic wooden cross held together by leather thongs claimed to mark the resting place of Kevin Carwell with the name and current year, 1853, carved roughly on the wood. Kevin suspected that it had been his dead friend Matt's sense of humor perhaps blended with regret. He realized that the legend might not be an exaggeration for very long. His stomach pain returned.

Kevin suspected that although the trio had found a way of hauling the treasure, they'd found it more practical to leave it to retrieve it later.

Bart laughed, "So that's where you jerks put all that shit!"

He quickly freed a shovel from a pack, dislodged the cross and with the shovel found a hard obstacle easily. He had been too excited to ask for help. The trunk hadn't been buried deeply, encrusted with dirt it was quickly exposed. The shovel used as a lever opened the container. Bart was distracted by its contents and let out insane peals of laughter. But he quickly recovered. Kevin judged that Bart's rifle secured to his saddle could not be reached fast enough.

Kevin and Agnes had to help him pack the money into sacks and load them onto the spare horses. Their task completed, Bart approached Kevin with long strides his Colt cocked in his hand.

"Your turn now, asshole!"

Kevin threw himself on the ground hoping at least to avoid a direct hit. A shot rang out. Bart was thrown backwards and held his abdomen in pain.

Without understanding what had happened Kevin hastened toward Bart to disarm him, but he was in the last throes of death.

Confused and surprised Kevin turned and saw Agnes next to the horses, cradling a rifle in her arms. Exactly what had happened?

"That's quite some shooting!" How do you thank a slip of a girl for saving your life?

He noted that she was trembling. Hastening to her side, he gently took the rifle and placed it on the ground. He hugged her with one arm. They were silent for some time.

There was no reason to tarry after burying Bart. Agnes began to speak as if there'd been no interruption.

"I was raised on a ranch."

"I'm glad you're on my side! Thank you for saving my life!"

"You don't watch a friend get killed." And after a pause, "And Rose is also my best friend."

They weren't quite finished. They had to go back to town. Kevin hated to think of the possible dangers, although nobody was likely to know what they were carrying. He couldn't keep one of his concerns to himself.

"Are you going back to Madame Bonjour?"

"That's all the family I got."

She must have noticed a disapproving tightening of his lips.

"I ain't going to be no whore."

"Any time you want to partner in a ranch, I'd be happy to accommodate you. I don't have the money yet but they posted a reward for returning this stuff and I certainly should share it with you."

Agnes smiled, an open amused smile, he had never seen before.

"You know damn well that it wouldn't work A man and a woman. You'd have to marry me and will have to wait a while for that."

Kevin found himself laughing. "So what they say about marriage and what women want is true!"

"You'll have to find out, won't you?"

TWILIGHT

In one of the seats in the middle of the crowd Sam had waited impatiently for Dona Stillwell's response to Eugene Spormann's speech. The applause after the incumbents's speech, had been enthusiastic. Still very popular, at least with that crowd, he obviously was the favorite candidate for the slot in the House of Representatives despite the obvious failures of his party still in power.

Sam had first become aware of Dona's existence when he had started gathering information for his Master's thesis on contemporary politics and their impact (or lack thereof) on people's lives. Later, after graduation he had become convinced that he needed to learn more about her. He had proposed an article for the Sunday edition of the local newspaper, "The Chronicle." Its text would examine the role of ideology on the political process. The editor was diffident. Sam suspected that he had been willing to consider the proposal only because Sam was the stepson of Albert Mirent, his uncle who had adopted him and who had been prominent in journalism circles. The editor's expression had shown no enthusiasm. His eyes behind thick glasses blinked and looked almost reptilian.

"Let's see what you can do. But keep in mind that if we don't accept it, we will be unlikely to consider any of your submissions."

In the discussion that Sam was witnessing, each candidate was supposed to simply present his or her views with no immediate rebuttal or an opportunity for questions. The arrangement had been chosen by Spormann's staff possibly because Stillwell was fast in formulating quick responses in an actual debate, whereas Spormann was not. Spormann, the scion of a politically successful family with high name recognition, could dictate his terms and didn't have to appear with his opponent at all. Stillwell was a newcomer to the political scene, a defender of the handicapped and the underdog, who in Sam's judgement had evolved into an interesting political figure in a national landscape of mediocrities.

The well-lighted hall had the anonymity of venues used for a variety of purposes. The smooth plain light gray walls were naked. Cameras from the local TV news were close to the podium. The three hundred or so people in the hall, probably a very partisan audience favoring Spormann, had found the proceedings sufficiently interesting to come.

On the podium, a pompous Mr. Blaufuss had presented a bland introduction before either speaker had started. He was supposed to enforce time limits, no more than forty minutes for each presentation as shown by a massive clock facing the audience. In the chosen format, each speaker could address the point of view of the competitor and Sam was sure that Stillwell would make a point of rebutting Spormann, point by point. She had been under attack on those very items and Sam knew she was sufficiently combative to take her opponent to task. Spormann had been forceful, logical and articulate, voicing opinions most of the crowd appreciated. Dignified, his gray hair beautifully coiffed, dressed in a dark suit and a red tie, he could be considered the perfect masculine specimen.

Sam had read everything about Ms. Stillwell he could find. Some of her speeches and talks, God knows why, had been recorded and were on tape. Her voice was sometimes light and humorous, but often unforgiving, uncompromising, mocking. She could be kind or she could be devastating. Her voice had a timbre he had learned to recognize and appreciate.

As a little girl her legs had been crushed in an accident, but she didn't make allowances for her handicap. Craning his neck to see her better, Sam was surprised to see her rise from her wheelchair and move nimbly on crutches toward the microphone with an unexpected swagger, perhaps to let everybody know that she was a presence to be reckoned with. Sam had seen films of FDR, his legs savaged by polio, where the man would part with whoever had offered him support and on his feet, on the podium would transform himself into a gladiator. Watching Stillwell he instinctively felt the same admiration he had felt for FDR's performance. He also thought her to be surprisingly attractive with a lovely smile, regular features and no-nonsense short chestnut hair. Before seeing her he had imagined her to be a much older woman, not in her early thirties as he guessed she actually was.

Her crutches were placed gently against the podium. Holding onto the lantern for support she proceeded with ease. Her presentation was without notes and each segment, each topic, started with a calm statement and then her response unfolded at an increasing tempo.

"Mr. Spormann, thank you very much for your presentation. I can't disagree with any of the principles you enumerated, but I really don't understand anything else you are trying to say … or perhaps you're just reciting a string of slogans."

"Marriage is sacred and should be strengthened. I couldn't agree more with Mr. Spormann. In this country, roughly 50% of marriages end in divorce. So much unhappiness! Don't kid yourself—I have never heard of a happy divorce. Roughly 40% of cohabiting heterosexual couples are not married. Perhaps my arithmetic is wrong, but doesn't that mean that as few as 30% of couples might be considered to have a "sacred" relationship? Shouldn't we worry about these facts which violate the crux of the supposed sacredness? Limiting marriages to heterosexual couples is supposed to bolster the sacredness of marriage. I would like to hear Mr. Spormann tell us why that is the case."

"Mr. Spormann is against abortions. So am I. It has been estimated that in America, 43% of women will have had at least one abortion by the time they are 45 years old. Do not underestimate the women's agony! It is imperative to do something about it. Only contraception can stop abortions. A resolute campaign to instruct and provide the means for contraception should be mounted. Some people equate abortions with murder. Why do they object to the use of contraceptives? Equating abortions to murder is absurd and by implication equating the use of contraceptive methods (such as condoms, diaphragms and the pill) with murder is criminal. Mr. Spormann and his friends have a surefire way of stopping abortions. They don't seem to be interested."

"Mr. Spormann is a conservative of the old school. I appreciate that. So am I. My dear grandparents, sadly now departed, were conservative. I learned my lessons from them. They saved every penny they could. Except under the most unusual circumstances, they considered going into debt immoral and I agree with them. They would have gone without eating before incurring debt! Yet they helped their children go through college as did my own parents. It's a question of how you spend your money. Why does a conservative tolerate a national debt of 8.3 trillion dollars and still mounting? Even more important, how is he proposing to repay it? I haven't heard anything about this from Mr. Spormann."

"Mr. Spormann is a conservative of the old school in other ways as well. So am I. It's good to conserve. I would like to hear him say how he's going to conserve the environment which is being ravished for the profit of the few who pollute us with mercury, carbon dioxide and PCBs."

"Mr. Spormann is patriotic. I appreciate that. So am I. I will not go into the pros and cons of war. I have spoken about that before. But what is patriotic about sending men and women into battle in too few numbers, ill-equipped and without the support or reconstruction of a country destroyed by war? War on the cheap is murder and murder of our own troops as well as the civilian casualties. Perhaps Mr. Spormann can explain what he has done to prevent this situation in his 10 years in Congress."

"Mr. Spormann loves children. So do I. Mr. Spormann has been blessed with three, and I believe one grandchild. I wish I had some of my own. It's good to be concerned about schools and it's important to be able to check on the progress of students all over the country and perhaps this can be done with a national test as done in the "No Child Left Behind" initiative. But doesn't it deserve an investment of our resources? It's our future we are talking about. The same can be said about colleges. What has happened to the American way of working your way through college? Presently, colleges are so expensive that students are forced to give up or go deeply into debt unless their parents are rich. Couldn't this be remedied by intelligent investment in education by our government? What has happened to our dreams of freedom and equality? Have they gone up in smoke like our other ideals? And what will our stinginess achieve especially regarding our competitiveness in the world markets in an increasingly technological world?"

Sam listened spellbound although he noticed the restiveness of some of the crowd. He remembered a saying he had read in the distant past: "Everybody loves the truth, but nobody wants to hear it."

Stillwell continued with more. Then she finished with a flourish and thanked the audience. There was polite applause by a few in the audience. Her presentation was not interrupted by the ringing of the monster clock as Sam had expected; Mr. Blaufuss fiddled with it to turn it off, Sam supposed. Stillwell shook hands with a smiling Spormann who had stood up and moved to where she had been standing. Then one of her helpers assisted her off the podium while another moved her wheelchair. A small group surrounded her with special questions. Sam held back diffidently. He didn't know exactly what he should say. She exited well after Spormann and his entourage. The crowd left mostly through the front door. She could operate her wheelchair by herself and she exited through a side door accompanied by a few supporters. Sam followed to intercept her before she disappeared into the night. He caught up with the small group in a well-lighted parking lot apparently reserved for guests and distinguished visitors. Another crowded parking lot where he had left his car was in front of the building.

"Great speech," he said. She looked at him coldly with little friendliness in her eyes. Her companions seemed to align next to or in front of her. "Oh, shit!" he thought "It's come to that."

"Who are you?"

"I'm Sam Mirent. I just want to exchange a few words with you. I'm an admirer of yours."

"You're a reporter?"

"Not exactly. Anyway, that's not why I'm here."

Sam seemed to have overstayed any possible welcome. He guessed that she had been subject to unpleasant encounters once too often. Four pair of eyes stared at him with intense dislike. "So, it's come to that," he thought again. Sam was prepared to retreat with at least some dignity when the situation suddenly changed. Three somber well-muscled men bearing baseball bats were lumbering toward them. One of them bellowed. "Go away slut! Go back where you came from!" They swung and smashed all the windows of two vans, the only vehicles left in the parking lot. With the shower of tiny of glass shards, Stillwell's group stepped back instinctively, leaving only Dona Stillwell in her wheelchair and Sam in front. Sam was terrified. His mouth had suddenly become dry and his heart accelerated to a rapid drumbeat. Suddenly anger overcame his fear. Glaring at the uninvited visitors, his hand grasped the inner pocket of his jacket. He was following the example of one of the scenes in the movie the "Godfather", when the Godfather was in the hospital without protection. He was surprised to see the trio suddenly split and run. Anger and bluff had done their work. He had been lucky to have decided at the last minute to dress more formally than usual. A jacket was not part of his favorite attire.

Dona seemed unfazed. The two of them looked at each other questioningly.

"Your car or mine?" asked Sam.

Dona burst out laughing. "Not much choice is there?"

"Well, I have to get it. It's parked in front. I don't know whether I can put your wheelchair in the trunk."

"It folds, you know."

"Anyway shouldn't you call the police? And what about your friends?"

"The police in this town? I don't think so. They would keep me here forever. I do have other commitments tomorrow. My friends will find their way to the hotel." When approached by a young attractive woman from her entourage she smiled at her. They had clearly been together for a long time. She didn't have to apologize. "I'm going to the hotel with Mr. Mirent. I'm sure AAA can tow your van and mine to be fixed. Take a cab after that. I don't want to stay in this town for very long. Unfortunately, we might have to leave tomorrow without the vans. It will be a bit difficult for all of us."

Sam was relieved that his car had decided to behave for a change. The battery had not discharged; it started without any trouble and the trip was smooth. At the hotel, he pulled out and unfolded the wheelchair. Strangely, helping Dona to exit and sit on the chair moved him. He felt very protective of her, although obviously she was far from helpless. The crutches were removed from the back seat and placed on the back of the wheelchair.

She asked, "Can I ask you in for a drink?"

Surprised, Sam accepted. "I'd be honored."

Dona operated the wheelchair with ease but then she said, "Please push me. That will guarantee more attention and perhaps faster service."

They sat at a table in a corner of the hotel's bar. But if he thought he was off the hook, he was wrong. With her face serious her queries started. "How do I know that you're not a reporter? Or for that matter a Spormann wannabe? And why did you follow me after the talk?"

"You wouldn't have come with me if you really had serious doubts about me. But I can't prove anything to defend myself. Why did I follow you? Well, that might be easier to explain. I was eager to meet you. Although I'm not a reporter I wanted to write something about people with the courage of their convictions. Your record intrigued me. I listened to all of your talks that have been recorded, some from your campaign for the handicapped and some of your political speeches as well. Let me say that I was immensely curious. Now that I found that you at least twenty years younger than I had guessed, I'm drawn to you as I would be to any attractive woman."

Suddenly overcome by an unfamiliar shyness, unable to sustain her stare, he looked away and missed the blush on her face.

"Please don't shit me with flattery. Courage my foot. And a cripple who can't stand on her two feet is not a woman a man could care for. Perhaps more a symbol of womanhood than a woman. And why should that make any difference?"

Surprised by her unsuspected insecurity, Sam looked up, "Let me be the judge of who's an attractive woman. That's one of the few things in which I'm competent! Of course it doesn't make a difference. I just was telling you what had an effect on me."

"Everybody must have some expertise in something or other." No longer in earnest, her laughter was quickly matched by his.

"If not exactly an expert on anything, I'm loyal, thoughtful, steady and reasonably endowed with common sense. You should be able to use me in your campaign. If working for you would produce a conflict of interest with my writing plans I'll just drop them."

"What's your political experience?"

"When in highschool I ran for class president and lost by a wide margin."

"Oh! That's a highly commendable!"

They were both laughing, but the anecdote helped her make up her mind. "Okay, let's give it a try!"

And that's how it came to be.

There were four volunteers managing Dona Stillwell's campaign, all young. Dona introduced them the following morning. Apparently, whenever possible they assembled each morning at breakfast to review what had happened the previous day and perhaps hatch a plan for the next few days. This time they reserved a room off the main dining room of the hotel.

"This is Sam who's going to help us. He has little experience so we need to direct him. Sam, we don't have a rigid organization. We help each other whenever it's necessary. Melissa mostly organizes meetings and schedules." Melissa in tight jeans and a cashmere sweater looked like the natural mate of Joe Cool, the legendary college playboy, except for her scowl; however, that quickly changed into a cheerful smile. "Abigail is our contact with the media and writes press releases." Dressed conservatively with a gray turtle neck and knee level dark skirt, her frequent smile looked too automatic to be spontaneous. Dona continued, "Sam might be able to help here too since he has some experience with newspapers." The only man in the group in jeans and t-shirt and a light vest also could have stepped out of college as he probably had. The twinkle in his eyes seemed to be a permanent fixture. "Tim is our masculine presence and muscle when it's not too hard. He's our supplier of unappreciated off-color jokes. And last, but not least is Samantha. She worries about my image, tells me when I'm doing a lousy job or when I'm totally removed from reality and makes overall plans. She is the closest thing to a manager and has to be tough." She quipped, "This gives us two Sams. How are we going to tell them apart?"

Tim chuckled seeming to affirm an accustomed role of wise guy and permanent teenager. "Why, that's simple enough. The one with the cute ass is our Sam!"

"God," Melissa piped in, "always with your mind in the gutter!"

"I wouldn't consider Sam in the gutter."

"Children! Children!" Samantha intervened, "Let's talk sense for a while."

They discussed their next stop, this time at a shopping center. They all would go in separate rented cars since their communal van still hadn't been repaired. Sam was supposed to follow them around and see what was happening. They broke up as a group to travel to the new locale and presumably take up their allotted tasks. By necessity Sam would drive Dona since they couldn't find a car properly equipped for the handicapped. Samantha managed to remain behind to have a last word with Sam. She grasped his arm to stop him. "Dona is too trusting. If I find out you're not on the level, I promise that you'll be more than sorry! So far I've only found that you have no police record and have a good credit rating, but these things don't mean much in today's cut-throat political world." Her severe expression complemented her words.

The threat sounded as if it was meant. Surprisingly Sam, who felt that hers were serious and reasonable concerns, found that he liked her forwardness and frankness. She was more attractive than he had first noticed. He knew well how susceptible he was to a pretty woman. Her eyes, he saw were of a green-blue combination. She had a clear complexion and light brown hair.

He tried to allay some of her reservations. "I'm what I say. You can count on it. I'll do everything possible for Dona's victory."

Samantha looked at him closely and had to ask, "Sam stands for Samuel or Samson?"

"Neither, Sam stands for Sam. Very respectable!"

Her suppressed chuckle was welcome. He would have hated to part on a somber note. She suddenly turned and with Sam followed the others.

Sam's position was very awkward—that of a stranger jumping into the middle of everything: no doubt arousing suspicions, no doubt stepping on toes of a group of proven loyalty and effectiveness. His first exchange with Samantha had already shown him that. But he felt he had to speak up at one of their meetings where they were reviewing their efforts. He had a totally different perspective from the others in the group.

"From what Dona has been telling me, I think you've done a very effective job. May I voice some ideas from my position as a new person?"

He felt unfamiliarly nervous without knowing why. Nobody dared to stop him but he could see from their expressions, that aside from Dona, their minds were closed. Retreating would lead him no place. At worse if he continued he might feel like an unmitigated fool—not an emotion he was unfamiliar with. He was willing to risk it.

"We should be able to capitalize on Dona as a person. She's young—has a magnificent smile—her crutches show she's gutsy. Not a bad quality in a Representative. We should make posters that show that and perhaps some very brief TV ads."

Sam noted that Dona's countenance had clouded. But to his surprise he found he had an unexpected ally in Samantha. Her face appeared to show that she was pleasantly intrigued.

He continued. "The ad and the posters should simply introduce a title appropriate for her speeches, to be delivered more as talks. On other occasions she has presented many outlining her positions. These include her take on how or whether government can be made to work. How youngsters can be made to learn by cooperating instead of competing. The need for preventive health care particularly of the young and many others. Then Samantha and Dona can work on these themes for short but effective talks from Dona's previous presentations. We can try to get her in invitations at various venues."

"Sounds expensive," Samantha said dreamily.

"Not really. The TV ads can be very, very short, with Dona just mentioning the topic."

"Getting the appropriate audiences for her presentations might be a problem."

"Curiosity raised by the TV ads may provide some. Certain audiences such as college kids have been neglected. An invitation from student groups or even the appropriate faculty might be finagled. There are four colleges in this district. I could take a crack at getting invitations. If Dona informs them while entertaining them, the audiences might grow. Most of the students are old enough to vote. In this state it's not too late to register."

Tim was leering. "There are some really cute chicks in those colleges."

Sam found the comment particularly inappropriate. On top of it, there were some cute chicks right there, but then he supposed by then they had become untouchable.

He could detect a tentative approval from Dona and enthusiastic support from Samantha and with their more overt backing, he decided to proceed. When he actually started on his quest for invitations, the effectiveness of their effort was aided by the presence of Melissa who volunteered to accompany him. Her attractiveness and apparent quiet allure opened many doors.

Visiting the student organizations, Melissa knew how to turn on the charm. Sam was ready when masculine solidarity was needed. Presenting some of Dona's ideas sometimes caught the students' imaginations and sometimes her less conventional approaches gave rise to enthusiasm. The administrators controlling student activities required a different approach. Generally, Sam would be wearing a suit and tie. Melissa and sometimes Samantha, also dressed conservatively, were demure and charming. What they stressed was the need to be open to new ideas and the suggestion that perhaps Spormann should also be invited. They were sure that Dona's opponent would spurn any invitation. His ideas were well known and his ads were all over the airways. Besides, his staff was not likely to follow up on those offers when so few votes were at stake.

A few meetings were arranged mostly at Community and other colleges. It was clear that Dona was a smashing success with students. She spoke to them with humor, as if they were equals, sharing a common sense view of the world and she never bored them. Some of the sophisticated political science students would elicit more detailed answers. It was clear that she was familiar with the politics of the House of Representatives, including specific bills which had been passed or rejected. In fact, her presentations acquired the reputation of scholarly analysis so that she was invited as a seminar speaker at State University.

Sam was rather intrigued by the depth of her knowledge. Samantha enlightened him. Dona had been part of Congressman Robert Greeves's staff both writing speeches and formulating bills. Greeves was one of the Congressmen in an adjoining district who had retained his seat over several elections.

Dona had been worried. "Something is wrong. Abigail has always been very punctual. She's been missing for all of yesterday. She would have called. Nobody answers her phone. Something very bad must have happened to her. You know where she lives, don't you Samantha? Can you go check? Take Sam with you. It may require two people."

The trip in Sam's overaged Toyota was uneventful—just direct highway travel. When they reached Hellerton, Samantha directed him through the maze of the local streets. The apartment house they stopped in front of was yellow brick and had a tired gray look. After one flight of stairs they reached Abigail's floor. Cracked in spots and faded in others, the blue door of the apartment needed a paint job. Aside from a tinkle from the inside of the apartment, there was no response when they pressed the bell. With no choice left they were prepared to leave when a male voice yelled, "Go away! Go away!"

Samantha intervened, "Please let us in if Abigail is there. We have been worried about her!"

"Get the fuck out!"

Sam decided to be more forceful. "If you don't open the door, we'll have to assume something is terribly wrong and call the police!"

"Oh, shit!" And the door opened a fraction on a chain. "She's fine. Go away."

The situation triggered something in Sam's mind. He kicked the door open so that the detached chain clanged and remained uselessly dangling with the door making vigorous contact with the man. Abigail was there alright, folded over on a sofa, her face swollen and black and blue. She looked terrified.

Sam's voice was threatening. "You're the boyfriend or husband, I take it."

"None of your business!"

"Now, how would you know if it's my business or not? Explain what happened."

The man took a swing at Sam. Sam's movements were like lightening. His right hand caught the arm and pulled the man's crotch onto Sam's knee, followed by a fist connecting to the face. The man went down bent over in pain. Sam held himself on the ready. Samantha held Sam's arm. "Please that's enough!"

But Sam wasn't finished with the man. "If you beat her up again, I'll be back and you'll wish you were dead."

Samantha reluctantly released his arm after discerning that the volcano was no longer erupting and took the few steps to get next to Abigail. On one knee, and holding her hand she asked, "Can we take you with us? You can stay in my apartment until you get better. We can take you to a doctor."

Abigail seemed in shock and was easily led to Sam's car.

When they reached the hospital there was a long wait. All sorts of people were in the ER waiting room. A young woman with straight black hair was trying to console a sobbing child. Unpleasant odors were emanating from a man in dirty rags. Three or four couples were waiting. Presumably a family member was inside being taken care of. When finally called, only Samantha was allowed to accompany Abigail.

She was warned, "You know, we'll have to report this to the police."

Samantha responded, "That depends on what she tells you, doesn't it? We just brought her here. We know nothing about what happened."

It was a while before they could take Abigail to Samantha's apartment. Except for the obvious bruises, there was nothing terribly physically wrong with her. No broken bones or concussion. She immediately stretched out on Samantha's bed. The shots to deaden the pain and the exhaustion from her beating were taking their toll. Samantha pulled Sam into the kitchen.

"You're a violent man. You can't do our cause any good. I'll have to ask Dona to drop you from our group."

"You might be right. I'm glad I did what I did, but to be frank I had little control over it. Something from my past took over. You don't have to talk to Dona at all, if that is your judgement I'll go my own way."

"So who was the victim before? Sister, friend, relative?"

"No, my mom. Please, I don't feel like discussing it."

He had thought that his early experiences had receded into a dense fog never to disturb him again. He remembered his fury without control. That's when his life had taken a sharp turn never to be the same again. His father's face appeared in front of him. Sam had never seen kindness in his features—the race for something always having precedence over anything else. A race for money, position, power. A wife who was too demanding. A son should be grateful for being born. The man had had other women in his life. When challenged by his wife all his brutality disgorged into violence. That's when something inside Sam had taken over.

"No! Don't you dare hit her again."

The first time Sam had been battered randomly by his father's fists. The second time, Sam had prepared carefully, training at a local martial arts school. He was the one doing the punishment; he could hear every sob shaking his mother while her soul was torn asunder.

Samantha found a friend who would stay with Abigail. There was only silence between Sam and Samantha as he drove to the hotel where their group was based.

Then Samantha broke the silence showing that her mind had been in overdrive. "How do you explain yesterday's episode when you hit the man with his Spormann picket sign."

"That's a different story. We were distributing leaflets in a public place, Woermer Plaza. Tim was carrying a box of leaflets. Melissa and I were ahead, trying to find a good place to put them down, out of the way. The man tried to block us. Melissa ignored him and pushed through. The man with the picket sign swung the damn thing at Melissa. I grabbed the pole or it would have split her head open. I did a bit of creative clumsiness and hit him in his belly with his own pole. I'm sure it looked perfectly legitimate—a simple attempt to deflect the sign. Some perceptive people might have realized it was deliberate but I imagine they would consider it a form of self-defense. It was calculated and coldly executed. With malicious intent. You judge what it means."

Silence returned for a while.

"Was that your dad … you know … who was being the abuser?"

"You ask too many questions. Once it cost me a tooth. The second time it cost me correctional school. You didn't find it when you checked me out because juvenile records are sealed."

At his point they had arrived at the hotel. She held him back with her hand as he tried to leave the car. "On second thought, I don't think I want you to leave our team. But you should be more careful. Acts of violence can have unpleasant consequences! I'll discuss it with Dona."

"Please do and make sure the two of you are right. There is too much riding on this."

"God! You don't want to make anything easy for us. Do you?"

Although still harboring strong reservations, Samantha was surprised to find that she actually liked Sam. Furthermore, she had been very conscious of the fact that he was a very desirable man. A long time had passed since she had been interested in men. He seemed to be pleasant, reliable, caring. Aaron Swinson III had cured her of any thoughts of romance for a long time. The pain from that encounter was still somewhere inside her ready to resurface, sometimes unexpectedly. Not all of her pain had been for nothing, perhaps it's what had changed her abruptly from a naive simple girl to a grown woman. In the process her interest in men and her faith in the human race had been weakened. She had centered all her love on Aaron. As difficult as it had been for her to cast aside her old-fashioned ideas, she had shared her bed with him for several months. He left at midterm when he graduated. He had assured her that he'd talk about the two of them with his family and they would become engaged soon. Just a month later, she was shocked in seeing in the "Northern News", the announcement of his engagement to a debutante. After that her pain didn't allow her to think properly. All those tender hours together must have had no meaning for him. Their dreams and thoughts about the future had been a simply a sham!

Her pain had been more than she could bear alone. Samantha had concluded that her parents couldn't possibly be of help or understand her situation and her emotional state. It had been lucky for her that her sister Alice had called her on the phone and had concluded from her choked words that something was very wrong. She insisted Samantha stay with her and her husband. The couple was still childless, making everything easier. At times of crisis Alice, five years older, had always been there for her. Never judgmental, she always had a way of seeing things from a very useful perspective. The calm routine of the couple's life and Samantha's being able to slowly tell her story to her sister bit by bit had a lot to do with her gradual recovery. Samantha felt that in that particular crisis, Alice may well have saved her life.

Back in college, keeping to herself and immersing herself in intense studies had turned her from a flighty and unsophisticated young girl into an accomplished scholar and researcher. She'd started on a new phase of her life when she met Dona and acquired a cause. In her experience Dona's mind and honesty had no equals.

Sam and all other members of the group were very pleased with the knew vigor and enthusiasm generated by their strategy of trying to carry their message to college audiences. That's not to say that more conventional means were neglected. Melissa had accepted an invitation by the township of Borton for Dona to debate Spormann. The concern of Dona's group was her health. The intensity of her speaking schedule was beginning to take its toll.

Not unexpectedly, the Congressman cancelled his appearance at Borton. He had been avoiding a face-to-face debate with Dona all along. The committee organizing the debate had decided that Dona could still present her views. Samantha and Sam were waiting in the parking lot for Dona to make her appearance when Samantha's cell phone indicated an incoming call with the sounds of the Woody Guthrie song "This land is your land, this land is my land …". At the other end, the hoarse voice hardly above a whisper was Dona's. She explained that her irritated throat had shown no signs of recovery. Could they please make her excuses with the audience? They shouldn't worry about her well being; Melissa could help Dona if she needed anything.

Sam and Samantha entered the building and looked over the crowd. The auditorium at Town Hall was full. In fact, some of the audience had liberated chairs from other rooms and had placed them wherever there was space in violation of fire rules. Sam estimated the crowd to be of sober and mature people.

Samantha asked, "Shall I or you announce the cancellation?"

"Why don't you give them a pep talk? Introduce yourself as Dona's right hand, explain our conundrum and offer to speak for Dona. You're as familiar with Dona's points of view and speeches as she is."

Gauging her reluctance he continued, "Why not? You're attractive. Smart. Articulate. Young beyond your years! We shouldn't lose this opportunity."

"Oh, Sam! I'm scared!" Then after a pause, "Do I look presentable?"

"You're perfect. Besides, your informal clothing will validate that this happened suddenly and without our knowledge. Let's step back into the corridor if you need to look at yourself in the mirror. Perhaps some lipstick?"

"Forget it! I don't carry any."

"Well, you look fabulous. Don't forget that I have heard you sound off before and I think you're great!"

Samantha walked on to the podium and smiled her great smile which seemed to encompass everybody present. She suppressed the memory, edging into her consciousness, of the presentation she once was supposed to give in high school, when she had frozen in front an audience.

"I'm Samantha Green. Some people say that I'm Dona Stillwell's right hand. Don't you believe it. I only carry out routine jobs. Dona only needs Dona. But on the other hand, I feel very close to her as if I were her sister, her little sister." Then she paused and projected a sad look. "I'm the bearer of bad news. After Congressman Spormann's cancellation, there is even more disappointment. I'm afraid you won't be able to hear Dona in person either. She has a serious case of laryngitis and she can hardly talk as we heard on the telephone a few minutes ago."

A disappointed collective "Oh!" greeted the announcement.

Samantha waited for silence and then continued. "I've been with Dona for a long time, while she was in Washington as assistant to Congressman Greeves and later when she headed the Foundation for the Disabled. She's known for her original ideas and her integrity. She's a terrific administrator—a courageous woman who has been at the cutting edge of great causes all her life. She is familiar with the many facets of Congress. She'd make a great congressperson."

"Today, she was supposed to talk about her vision of how our government can be made to work. If you wish I can present her views and then answer questions. I know I must be a disappointment. I'm not as smart or as earnest as Dona but I'll have to suffice if you wish me to continue with my most fervent apologies for her absence."

Some people left with the scraping of chairs but many voices were raised, "Please stay!" "We want to hear!"

After flashing her powerful smile, and again waiting for silence, Samantha continued. Although her voice sounded years younger, her style was similar to that of Dona. First she calmly laid out the terrible state of today's government and its bureaucracy one item at a time and then continued at an increasing tempo offering various solutions for each problem, some rather painful but still necessary.

At the end the applause was enthusiastic and Samantha's face was flushed with pleasure. Sam joined her for the questions but his presence was totally unnecessary. She handled herself with charm, sometimes firmly, sometimes accepting that the opinion she had just heard was important and she would convey it to Dona.

Sam didn't know what triggered his response when they were in the corridor. "You were magnificent. And I think you're the most beautiful woman in the world!" He meant every word and he kissed her. Not an innocent kiss but a passionate kiss. Even more surprising she seemed to reciprocate.

Before Sam had a chance to start the car their passions escalated.

"Don't just sit there, you big palooka. I rate at least another a hug!"

Sam held her in his arms and kissed her face all over. She snuggled inside his arms but didn't seem satisfied. "Just like that, eh? Shouldn't there be some words accompanying that?"

"You were magnificent. And don't expect me to say that I love you because that would be inadequate. I adore you. Furthermore, I'd love to get you into bed as soon as possible." And he realized that he meant every word.

She let him accompany her to her hotel room. Melissa who was sharing the room with her was fortunately not there. They embraced again passionately, body tight against body, mouth and mouth in intimate contact. His hands descended to her breast, then to her behind.

But then she broke apart suddenly. "You know we can't let anything like that happen. At least not until after the election. Please! Now we know what we feel about each other, we can wait."

"The voice of reason in the most beautiful body I've ever seen. You're right and I'll keep my feelings to myself. But I'll be ready for you just after the vote count is completed."

The world had taken a rosy turn. Sam was suddenly happy with what had happened between him and Samantha, as well as his work with Dona and his new friends. But unexpectedly Sam's world collapsed.

The blinking light on the phone in his hotel room indicated that a message had been left. Dona's voice, stern and angry, didn't bode well. She summoned him. He couldn't help being concerned. This wasn't her style. Had a crisis appeared on the horizon? Figuring that his dalliance with Samantha, if it could be called that, was to be questioned, Sam calmed down. He was ready to confess. "Sorry, I just fell in love with her. I couldn't help it. I can hold my impulses back until the election is over."

After knocking on her door and entering, he knew that he was facing some other kind of crisis. Both Dona and Samantha were there. Although Dona's expression showed no emotion, Samantha's face emanated only hate. What was going on? He had thought that she at least was fond of him. Samantha's voice attacked him. "I told you that if I found out you weren't on the level you'd be more than sorry!"

"Oh, shit, are we back to that!"

"I found out you're Harlon's son."

A few moments of silence followed. He was nonplused. It had been such a long time since he'd thought of himself as Harlon's son that he never thought it would become an issue. "Well, that I am. He's my biological father. You must have also found out that my name was changed by a court order at my request when I reached the age of eighteen. I wasn't exactly hiding it but I certainly felt it wasn't a recommendation."

"Yea, sure. Look at this." And she handed him a newspaper. The headline stated "National party spokesman, Joe Harlon, to take over as Spormann's campaign manager."

"Is it a coincidence that the opposition's master of dirty tricks is now facing us just when the polls showed that we are neck and neck with Spormann? And is it a coincidence that you have been hitting on both me and Dona?"

He was silent until he could put his thoughts together. "Don't be so simpleminded. I was just flirting with Dona. It seems to me she never thought of herself as an attractive woman which she is. I wanted to change her self-image. Dona never took my attentions seriously. Look, I did a damn good job for your campaign. Would I have done that if I were with the opposition?"

"Sure, and any advantage we have can be wiped out in a second if Harlon finds out about what was going on between you and the two of us and starts one of his ugly rumors."

"True enough. But there is no reason he'd find out about our quarreling trio unless he was tapping your room and heard this conversation."

"Or you told him. And you could easily provide false testimony about our group."

"Hold off!" It was Dona's turn to intervene. "Samantha, you're jumping to conclusions and the campaign is almost over. So far I think Sam has explained himself well. We have no evidence of maliciousness."

"Dona, you're too soft-hearted! Either he leaves or I leave. I have been your right hand for years and if you win you'll have to face a term in Congress without me."

"Just a minute, please." Sam held up his hand and knew what he had to do. "My role in the campaign is almost over. Why don't I just make myself scarce. If I'm the bastard Samantha thinks, the damage has been done. If I'm sweet, loyal Sam, I'm not needed anymore; we are only ten days from the election. If you need me for a new crisis you can call me at home."

Sam was determined not to show the intense pain he felt. The two women were speechless. He bowed ironically and left feeling that his heart was going to break. The price of falling in love, he thought.

Yes, indeed, Harlon was his biological father but Sam certainly didn't feel that way. Sam remembered well his last days at the correctional facility which had eventually defined his future. He had worried about what would happen when his two years were over. While confined, his mother had died in an unfortunate automobile accident. He had been assured her death had been instantaneous. Overwhelmed by grief, he had been allowed to go to the funeral accompanied by one of the supervisors.

The proceedings had been somber. He'd recognized some of the neighbors, although their condolences and declarations hadn't helped him much. The minister's eulogy had made it clear that he hardly knew the deceased. He met his uncle Albert Mirent, whom he hardly knew, for the first time after many years. He had made the funeral arrangements. They shook hands. Sam was relieved that he didn't hug him and even more that his father had not attended. Hypocrisy was not one of his faults.

Somehow the ceremony had not given him closure. Nothing could abate his pain or feelings of guilt. Not having been there for his mother at least for a while before her death was really overwhelming.

Aside from being confined, his two years had not been completely unpleasant. His stay was quickly defined by an episode involving a muscle-bound bully, Dirk. He'd harass Sam but usually in full view of monitors and other boys. Sam hadn't felt threatened and he could take ridicule without showing resentment. Being cornered in a dark spot was another matter. Dirk came at him with a belligerent look. "You've been fucking little boys, haven't you? That's why you're here."

Sam took measure of the situation. Dirk was fully grown and over six feet tall; he had at least thirty pounds on him. He waited until Dirk was just a few feet from him, fists raised. His right foot hit Dirk's right knee and turning into him, Sam flipped him. The floor shook from his fall. He was lucky after that. Dirk and the monitor were not interested in having the outcome known to the administration or the rest of the boys. So Sam wasn't punished. He would have been very concerned if they had added a few months to his stay. Dirk needed some complex surgery to his knee and a period of rehabilitation.

After the incident with Dirk, he was left alone. He found that the school program of the facility was one way of keeping his mind from boredom and eventually was the reason why he could continue his life on an even keel when he later attended a regular high school.

Sam was afraid that upon his release he would be in his father's custody. During the hearing, the judge had listened to Sam's account, nodded thoughtfully and delayed his release for a long week. Sam, distrustful of bureaucracy, was sure that something had gone completely awry. Again interviewed by the judge, the jurist asked him whether he'd accept custody being granted to his maternal uncle, Albert Mirent. He must have volunteered to accept the responsibility. Sam didn't know him well since he hadn't lived in the same city. His mother had always spoken affectionately of him. Sam knew he was married and had a daughter close to his age. He must be a good guy or he wouldn't have volunteered. Accepting him was certainly a way of terminating the impasse.

Sam found his uncle taller than he'd remembered. Dressed formally in a suit and blue tie, his bright blue eyes that with a stab of pain reminded Sam of his mother. Dignified, his gray hair's composure was disturbed by a cowlick grazing his forehead.

They were soon on their way. The discord of sounds at the airport was a new experience. The security measures that had been touted by the news media didn't alarm him. It was reminiscent of the count and searches he had become familiar with. The airplane trip, his first, was short. His many worries marred any wonderment he might have felt.

His uncle, sitting next to Sam, bent toward him. "You'll like your Aunt Amantha. She loves children and even teenagers! And everybody needs a sister! They have a way of taking one down a peg when necessary. And they are indispensable at other times as well. You'll like Patricia, she is close to your age, although she's a prickly cactus, a bit like you, but of course they are different prickles!" And after a long pause, "I was fortunate with mine, your mother. We all miss her terribly."

They didn't talk much after that. Sam thought that his uncle was wise to leave him with the thoughts and concerns crowding his mind. What would his new family be like? He had forgotten the meaning of family life. What would school be like?

He really became part of the family when he reached an accommodation with his Cousin Patricia.

Sam had never had a second chance before and a third chance was too much to expect. Patricia had made one of her hateful comments. Teasing him seemed to be something his fourteen-year-old cousin enjoyed. "I wouldn't expect an insensitive jerk like you to understand. You're just like your father."

They had just met a few days before and already he'd had to bear her sarcasm and innuendos. This comment had touched him deeply. He slapped her. It was lucky that something inside him held him back to soften the blow. She stepped back with tears of anger. It was then that he realized what had happened and what it might mean. One way or the other, he would be thrown out onto the street physically or figuratively. For the first time he had experienced the beginning of a life with family and warmth surrounding him. And that was likely to end. Besides, he doubted she had deserved such a violent response. Hers was a world of words and word games. Much different from the one he had experienced. There was a double irony in what had happened. Hitting her was probably a response his father was capable of. As irritating as she was, basically he realized he did care for her. His uncle had warned him that everybody needed a sister to teach them humility, and suddenly he understood what he'd meant.

He felt tears crowding his eyes, hugged her knowing that wasn't enough—neither were his words. "I'm sorry, I'm sorry. You touched a nerve. I'm a total jerk. I didn't want to hurt you. Please forgive me!"

Rigid, rejecting his hug, she suddenly pushed him back. "You asshole! Don't ever hit me again!" She turned down his offer to get some ice. "No need." Her teasing spirit surfaced again. "It wasn't that bad. You're not the strong virile guy you imagine." Then she laughed. It was over. She never mentioned the incident again.

The Mirents introduced Sam to a world unknown to him. It wasn't hard to take to Aunt Amantha, a cheerful and affectionate woman, even toward the most recent addition to the family. She was always ready with an encouraging word and sensitive to Sam's feelings. The interaction between the three was even more revealing. The arguments were frequent but good-natured and the outcome always well thought out if the issue was significant. Although Patricia was a mistress of the needle, always well aimed at Sam, he quickly grew to like her. He understood his Uncle's remark about her prickles.

Getting accustomed to the school was not difficult. Initially he was embarrassed by the presence of Patricia, who was in his class. He was quickly put at ease when he found out that whenever somebody teased him, Patricia was ready to demolish the offender with some of her well-chosen words. He found that he had been well prepared by the school of the correctional institution and didn't have to worry about the difficulty he might encounter.

After leaving Dona's group, he tried to start life again by returning to his apartment. The disorder in his office was daunting. Strewn on his desk, several cut up articles from newspapers stared at him. No less than two notebooks had notes that he couldn't even decipher. He always preferred to put his thoughts in writing in the old-fashioned way, with pen and paper rather than on a computer. He examined the notes for the article he had written before meeting Dona and Samantha. Unfortunately, the ability to concentrate seemed to have deserted him. He figured he might as well watch what was happening in Dona's campaign. It was worrying him. He wondered what dirty trick Harlon was cooking up. Sam couldn't help it; his loyalty remained with the two women even if they had rejected him.

It didn't take long for Harlon to strike. A rumor that half a million had disappeared from the Foundation for the Disabled Dona had headed before her resignation to start her political campaign was reported. Sam refused to get excited. His belief in Dona was unequivocal. She was a straight arrow and nobody would have been able to put something like that over during her leadership. But of course demonstrating that there was no basis for the accusation wasn't that easy. He put his feet up on his desk and tried to relax as much as possible. The feeling that old man Harlon had lost his touch kept coming back to him as he considered the situation. There wasn't much time to dispel the rumor, but eventually the falseness of it would become evident and if the source traced could destroy Harlon's reputation as the magic man unless it actually worked. Deflecting the blow by unearthing the facts unfortunately would take time and the election was just a few days away. It occurred to Sam that one dirty trick deserved another. Feints in chess and martial arts had a way of working. Perhaps the skill to conceive and implement them was inherited. What would people conclude if they found out that Harlon's own son had been embedded in Dona's camp? Wouldn't that be taken as proof of dirty tricks. It amused him to think the very fact that had viciously hurt him could now be used for Dona's cause.

There were three people he could always count on, the Mirents. He phoned Patricia, who was now on the staff of Channel 6 News, and than his Uncle, Albert Mirent. The ploy had a good chance of working. Albert listened to him carefully and assented but he told him, "This might work or it might not. It might also hurt you."

The counterpunch was quick. When the media found out that Harlon's son had been on the staff of Dona Stillwell, they quickly picked up the bait and strongly hinted that he must have been in cahoots with his dad and part of a conspiracy to damage Stillwell. The news quickly overwhelmed the other rumors. After all, this was a fact that couldn't be denied and they could discuss and argue about it *ad infinitum.*

Sam made a point of disappearing completely and the media were unable to find him and interview him. This fanned the flames of suspicion even more. Good, Sam reflected, sometimes good can come from bad.

To his delight, Dona Stillwell won by two hundred and forty four votes out of forty thousand. A recount confirmed the results. Something had gone right. He wasn't sure whether his trick had helped, but he was delighted by the out-come. Sam found out the results by calling his Uncle. Now he could rest and resume his life. Of course, by then the whole mise-en-scene had collapsed. There was no money missing. The rumor of the missing funds was traced to Spormann's aides and the danger was over. There were many unanswered questions but by then the media quickly returned to more recent and juicier scandals.

❦   ❦   ❦

Several weeks had gone by when his doorbell rang. Sam felt like ignoring its summons. He was working. As unsatisfied as he was with his writing, it was still work. But perhaps with an interruption he would regain some momentum. He succumbed to the desire to delay his writing. He opened the door. Samantha's presence on his doorstep jolted him. She was as speechless as he was. It took him a few moments before he could find the strength.

"Please come in."

He pointed at a chair that wasn't covered with papers, newspaper cuttings and notes.

Samantha broke the silence. "I suppose I should have called first but I thought you might not want to see me." And after a long pause, "Dona asked me to talk to you. Didn't you get her invitation?"

"I haven't been looking at my mail for some time. I just pile it up on a chair. All I'm expecting are bills."

"She's getting married and she invited you to the wedding."

"I'm not sure I should attend. But for goodness sake, who is she marrying?"

For the first time a smile came to her lips. "Bob Greeves of course. The representative she had been working for. They are practically soul mates and luckily he was reelected. He's been in love with her for a long time. For a long time, she thought he was just feeling sorry for her. Now, they are both ecstatic. You wouldn't even recognize her! Please come to her wedding. It means a lot to her. Remember, she always was on your side. She thinks you had a lot to do with her change of attitude."

"Well, I'll consider it."

"Sam, please go. I'm the villain of the piece, not her. If you attend, I'll be as inconspicuous as possible." After a long pause. "I'm sorry. I was wrong and all I can do now is apologize. I have been in love only twice in my life. The first time, the man was a horror. The second time I screwed up. Getting nasty with you was the most painful thing I have ever done. I thought I had to do it. Don't think I didn't guess later about the ploy you engineered. I think it turned the tide. I know fully what we and I owe to you."

"The fault is not all yours. I should have confided in you, but everything happened so quickly! We were lovers for how long? One night? Forty minutes? Not enough to exchange any meaningful personal information. Well that's the past. Are you going to Washington with Dona?"

"No, I think it best if I stick around."

"That doesn't make any sense."

"Sam, please don't get mad at me. I know I don't deserve it and I'm just dreaming. I would like to stick around until I'm sure I don't stand a chance with you."

They were both motionless for a few seconds. "Samantha, your turning against me hurt me. But what happened is not surprising in this day and age where treachery and opportunism seem to prevail. Your suspicions were logical. I never loved anybody as much as I love you. I think it would be foolish if we didn't give it a try. Would you go to Washington if I came along?"

There were tears in her eyes and she didn't have to answer. They kissed gently, lovingly. He felt her trembling in his arms and knew everything was going to be alright.

THE BURGLAR

Alice Horwell had watched the sunset with some enjoyment, some trepidation—the sun disappearing behind rose clouds and the profile of the mountains outlined by the rapidly disappearing light. Night had been about to envelope her in loneliness. She was supposed to attend a church function and had even baked cookies for the occasion, but a hurried telephone call from Millie Desposs had informed her that it had been cancelled. And so she was alone in the dark when she could least tolerate it.

She felt despair compounded by fear. Alone in the middle of the night in a house too large to be comfortable—too luxurious to be her home. Abandoned by her husband, Herbert, who was indifferent to her. Spent so little time with her—it hardly mattered if he was kept away by indifference or another woman. That was her despair. And then there were noises she couldn't identify, the cause of her fear. She felt subtle changes in drafts that she hadn't noticed before. She had the feeling she wasn't alone in the house. Yet every door, every window had been locked. Was it her imagination fueled by her unhappiness and loneliness? Or was the creaking on the stairway somebody moving about? Was the tinkle of glass a window being broken to enter the locked house? Or was it just the wind playing on a chime. Did they even have a wind chime? Perhaps Herbert had put one up without telling her. They exchanged so few words between them when they were together. Alice was afraid of initiating one of his litanies which would leave her stripped of dignity and self-respect. So she never criticized, never expressed her honest opinion.

Herbert, in her mind no longer Herbie, was undermining her self-confidence—her self-respect. Why was she so dumb? Even a child could understand what he was saying. She was getting fat—she should eschew the chocolate she was so fond of. Didn't she have any self-control? The dress she wore at the country club party was in such bad taste that he had been embarrassed. All seemed rationalizations to justify infidelity or a divorce to come.

There was an unmistakable creak of somebody in the hallway. In their better days Herbert had shown her the Baby Browning he kept loaded in a drawer of the coffee table. For protection, he had said, and he had shown her how to use it. Until this moment, to her the miniature handgun was just a toy. She went to the drawer and quickly had it in her hands. Its possession failed to reassure her.

Suddenly, a shadow parted from the darkness of the doorway. A click activated the room light. For a moment she was almost blinded although she could see a man in front of her. The intruder had no weapon or mask He quickly took shape in her mind as her eyesight adjusted—not anybody she knew. Fear enveloped her. He was an ordinary man. Dressed entirely in black, his face with a small straight nose and his fair hair were like that of many other men she had seen before. She hoped he was just a burglar, not somebody more intent on hurting her. In her estimation all men had become sadists and criminals.

He laughed. "You were supposed to be away!" And after an instant, "Don't get excited. I mean you no harm. Please give me that gun."

She had often wondered whether she had the guts to shoot an intruder. She closed her eyes as her fear took over, past any logical thought. Her heart beat accelerating, and her mind reaching the level of hysteria, she pressed the trigger repeatedly. But nothing happened. After a few long steps, the intruder grabbed the gun out of her hand and somehow made it disappear.

"You left the safety on." His amused voice had an element of a didactic, disapproving tone. "But it doesn't matter. I have no evil intent except a bit of larceny. You're rich. It won't make much of a difference to you or your husband." Pointing, he then continued, "Sit on that chair. I don't want to threaten you or tie you down. But I will if I have to."

She felt as if she were in an impossible nightmare—not sure whether he was just trying to calm her with some intent other than theft in mind. Rape seemed unlikely although that would have been the ultimate injury to her self-respect. She had had similar bad dreams before, but she also knew that what she was witnessing was reality. It also came to her mind that many criminals sound gentlemanly, some had even become legends, but criminals they still were and could be vicious. She sat as he had suggested and didn't move.

Those big eyes, like those of a child, but clouded by fear were staring at him. The intruder almost felt sympathy for her. In the past, he himself had known fear. He suppressed a strong urge to reassure her further.

His eyes kept going back to her and she knew that even if he hadn't been before, he was now armed and could harm her even at a distance. He detached a painting from the wall. Some modern monstrosity that only Herbert could like. There was a small safe behind it. She had known about it since it had been installed, although she didn't know the combination. It contained a large amount of cash; Herbert was very mysterious about its other contents. The intruder turned the dial and easily opened it. He must know the combination. How did he manage that, she wondered? Some packets and sheets of paper were transferred a few at a time to a black sack attached to his waist.

The man turned around and in silence quickly disappeared through the open doorway from which he had come. Alice didn't know what to make of it. Her mind had too much to deal with. Nevertheless, she no longer felt threatened and her heart slowed down to a more normal pace.

🍁   🍁   🍁

A few days later, the telephone rang. Alice was ready to hang up if it was Herbert again ready to berate her. The voice wasn't his. For some reason it sounded familiar.

"You didn't call the police."

Only after understanding the words did she deduce that the caller must be the polite burglar. It took her a moment to orient herself. Why in the world was he calling her for? Why did she feel compelled to explain? The moment in time they had shared hadn't made them comrades. Her impulse to elaborate made her feel foolish.

"What would have been the point? I couldn't have been personally involved. I don't know the combination of the safe! All I know is that my husband, or should I say my pre-ex-husband, became hopping mad to find it empty but still didn't inform the police. I have no sympathy for him or his confusion. Anything I could have said wouldn't have filled any useful purpose. Herbert has started divorce proceedings. Time for him to do without my help."

🍁   🍁   🍁

Although she had completely accepted the idea of a divorce, she still had been reluctant to be present when a financial settlement was discussed. She thought it would hurt. A romance and then its failure ultimately reduced to considerations of cash. But she didn't have much choice in the matter. Her lawyer had insisted.

"I'm going to get the meanest Jewish lawyer I can get and you won't get a penny," Herbert had threatened.

The irony was that his lawyer, Johnson, wasn't Jewish, but hers, Bart Treifuss, was and was one of the sweetest men she knew—probably without an ounce of meanness in him. When it was too late, she'd thought that it's always a mistake to hire a lawyer who's a friend. In addition, Bart was generally reluctant to take on divorce cases. He claimed he shared too much of the pain. But then a childhood friend can't be easily turned down.

They were sitting at a table in Johnson's office with her and Treifuss on one side and Herbert and his lawyer on the other.

"Since there is no child support to be discussed," Johnson was affirming pretentiously, "I'm afraid you'll find that Mrs. Horwell is entitled to very little, particularly since Mr. Horwell's company is now bankrupt and his estate is minimal."

Bart as usual appeared ineffectual. He smiled a sweet shy smile and blinked behind his thick glasses. "I beg to differ." All he did was hand a stack of papers to Johnson.

Johnson looked at the material, at first superciliously, but then his expression seemed to change. Without a word he handed the material to Herbert, who turned purple.

"How the shit did you get these?"

Johnson ignored the outburst and softly addressed Bart. "What do you propose?"

Alice was to remember little of the exchange that followed except that the settlement was good. She couldn't help asking after they left. "What in the world was that all about?"

"A photographic record of all Herbert's accounts and transactions, some of which the IRS would love to see."

"How did you get them?"

"They came by special messenger a few days ago. I have no idea who sent them. They had a note along with them. It said, "From your friendly burglar." As if that were possible! I thought at first that they were a joke but then I checked each one."

Alice felt that it had been very strange from the moment Herbert had decided on a divorce to when the burglar had entered her life.

THE FOOL

There is nothing more humiliating for a fool than to realize he is one. He had thought of her, Lillian Bartholomew, as a slip of a woman. Attractive, although not so young anymore. Perhaps her maturity had been an added attraction. A full figure and expressive dark eyes. Blonde hair beginning to show a few gray strands. Well-spoken and always sensitive to his moods. Everett Pollington had made millions handling mergers, acquisition, sales. The last movie he had produced had made millions. But he hadn't seen her trap until it was sprung.

The affair had been very pleasant. The sexual encounters showed that her skills and experience were considerable. Angry as he was after finding out that she had taken advantage of him, he still felt a quickening when he thought of their affair. He had known that for years she had been the girlfriend of a well-known millionaire who eventually had dumped her as had been reported gleefully by the gossip mongers of the press and television. In fact when Everett had first met her he had been in full sympathy with her. At that time he had felt she hadn't deserved the humiliation.

But then he had been played for a fool. She'd claimed to have become pregnant and maintained that he was the father. He'd rejected the claim. In this day and age you get pregnant mostly when you want to. A good deal of mutual name calling had followed. Eventually, he had been humiliated by the appropriate DNA test and exposed for the fool he was. The child was his. Furthermore, he officially became the father of the little girl. There was a reason why he hadn't gotten married. He hadn't been ready for fatherhood or firm ties.

His mistake had cost him a considerable amount of money for the upkeep of mother and child. It had all been handled through lawyers and his had been too generous, misinterpreting his well-known benevolence in other matters such as his philanthropies.

Months after the birth of the baby and the financial settlement, Lillian had insisted on trying to talk to him. He saw no reason to rehash their conflict and to avoid her calls had changed his home telephone number to an unlisted one. Shortly after that she'd started to call him at his office. The layer of secretaries required by his exalted status and headed by his indispensable Ms. Plum didn't have much trouble shielding him, but it still was a nuisance.

One day he had stayed late at work and had made the error of picking up the phone.

"Everett, I really have to talk to you."

For some reason he was only mildly irritated. You had to give her credit for her persistence.

"Talk to my lawyers but you're not going to get any more money out of me."

"Yes, you were very generous. That's not what I want to talk about."

The cadences of her voice were melodious. She had a lovely voice.

"What could you possibly want to talk about?" She had peaked his curiosity. And perhaps he could put an end to her badgering.

"I would like to meet you somewhere. I promise no recriminations, just talk. I don't want to do it on the phone."

They met at an out of the way coffee shop. Fortunately nobody recognized him. He thought she should have chosen a place with a less bright environment to be less conspicuous. She was late as usual, of course. She was dressed simply in jeans and a basic blouse. All the same she still attracted attention. Just what he didn't want. He was tired of seeing his woes displayed in newspapers stories or in the sarcastic accounts of television commentators. He felt a wave of resentment come forth. That wouldn't do. He had learned in his business dealings that emotions just interfere with his performance and what could this be but a business deal?

She looked at him seriously. "Thank you for meeting with me, Everett."

"Don't think that I have made peace with you. I think what you did was contemptible."

"I understand, Everett."

The waiter approached them and they ordered just coffee. She waited until the two cups were placed on the table. "I thought it might hurt you less if you knew what had gone through my mind during that period." She stopped for a while. "You might remember that our affair started without warning. I was counting on the morning-after pill to do its work. But later I thought, 'I have wanted children for several years and I had been denied that possibility. Why not just let it happen.' I'm not that young anymore and I still didn't seem to have learned to pick a man capable of commitment. Money had not been on my mind. In fact, I really didn't know you were that "Everett Pollington." When my pregnancy advanced, I told you about it. It may seem silly to you but your denial hurt me. Besides, why shouldn't I have taken advantage of the situation. I could guarantee the comfort of my child … and of course mine. It might all have been contemptible but I don't regret what I did. I'm sorry if I hurt you."

Everett forced himself to show no emotion. Of course that was how she would see it.

"There is an added feature," she continued. "I'm providing you with a child with no involvement on your part. No diapers, crying at night, worries when she's sick. Although I wish you would at least see her. She's so loveable! As you get older, her presence will make a difference to you and I promise that I'll make sure that she'll respect you. If you want her to love you, you'll have to work at it. That's really all I have to say."

They remained silent sipping their coffee. "I really didn't want this!" she said amused pointing at the coffee.

"Well you have had your say. I hope you'll stop badgering me."

She seemed disappointed. He wondered what she had expected. "If that's what you want, you will not hear from me again," she answered.

❦   ❦   ❦

Everett's time was taken up by the various activities of Pollington Enterprises. He had been about to enter in a new venture—purchasing a hotel chain in Florida. He had little experience with real estate and none in hotels, so he approached the possibility with good deal of caution. Digging out the information and evaluating the findings were time-consuming and required a good deal of concentration. His faithful secretary, Ms. Plum, who always saw only his side and could be quite vengeful, broke his concentration.

"You know that Bartholomew woman finally got what she deserves. She's been in a car accident. Nothing fatal. Unfortunately her little girl is very sick—I hope the little innocent recovers."

He couldn't figure out why he was so disturbed. He must be entirely addled. He broke off the negotiations and was in an airplane heading for New York in no time at all.

He had never seen Lillian's new apartment. Its lusciousness showed him that it must have taken a good deal of the monthly settlement. The doorman was reluctant to let him go up and it was only after contacting the apartment that he consented in letting Everett through.

The woman who came to the door might have been a nurse or just a helper. A door opened and Lillian appeared. One of her arms was bandaged and one of her legs was encased in a cast. "About time you discovered how to be a human being, if you came to help."

Everett nodded. Entering the room from which Lillian had appeared, for the first time he saw his daughter, Miriam. Although clearly not at her best, with fever ravishing her, there was no question that she was a pretty child.

He was confused about what happened next. He found himself holding the baby. Changing her after receiving proper instructions. Rushing to the drugstore to get something that he didn't even know what it was. The male doctor, with the usual chauvinism, seemed to favor addressing him rather than Lillian. Everett couldn't help seeing the undisguised smirk on Lillian's face. For him it was an entirely new experience.

When Miriam recovered, his last visit seemed to be a time to celebrate. The only appropriate drink Lillian had in the apartment was an unpretentious New York State white wine and they toasted to Miriam's health sitting side by side. His presence seemed to be very natural.

"Will you let me visit Miriam?"

"I wouldn't think of stopping you even if you really don't deserve it." She laughed. "Besides you could get a court order easily enough!"

They sat in silence for some time. He was reluctant to go, she was reluctant to end their celebration.

He proceeded shyly without knowing where his impulses were leading him. "Have you taken up with anybody yet?" It seemed a natural assumption. He had always known that there was something about her that made her remarkably attractive. But he had no idea why he was asking.

Lillian laughed, "Who wants to get saddled with a woman with a baby? Not very enticing. And I certainly didn't get a chance to be socially active. As you saw, Miriam is a handful even with all the domestic help I have. You, of course, must have taken up with one of the many nymphettes that crowd around rich men."

Martin knew that she was right, but he never had felt attracted to any of those women. Lillian certainly hadn't seemed to have any of their traits.

It was his turn to laugh. "How could I possibly have gotten involved so soon. After all, I got into trouble with my last involvement and made a vow to be more careful. Besides, making money is very demanding. I had to give up a possible lucrative deal to purchase a chain of hotels to come here when you were in the car accident and Miriam got sick."

"Oh! Poor baby. I feel so sorry for you! You missed a few millions!"

Again there was a period of silence.

"Look. We know each other very well. All our warts and quirks. Can we see each other again?"

"Oh! My poor Everett. You just can't express yourself. You mean, can we become lovers again?"

Everett nodded and was blushing like a high school boy.

"What a preposterous idea, after all our name calling!"

"As I said, knowing all our warts and quirks."

"Everett, you know a lot more about me now. I told you I wanted children and I'd failed in the conventional avenues. We'd be back in the same situation." Then after a pause she continued. "I imagine I could get pregnant from a sperm bank but I'd prefer the old-fashioned way and I would prefer it if the siblings had the same father."

"Would you at least consider it?"

"We probably would fight like cats and dogs."

He took her hand. "It might be worthwhile." For some reason he felt moved. All he saw on Lillian's face was amusement.

DOUBTS AND CERTITUDES

Martin was unaccustomed to solemnity and dramatic moments. Yet that was what was facing him. The sober man confronting him, Cyril Appleton, was what you might expect in a lawyer who represented not just the rich and famous, but also the ones whose families had held money for generations, Martin imagined. Middle-aged, tall and spare, Appleton had thinning graying hair on his crown combed tight against his skull. His suit was dark and well cut. His tie was red silk with a distinctive Italian design. He was sitting behind a polished walnut desk of exceptional size. His revelations had an almost biblical impact on Martin. Martin with tousled hair, jeans and sweatshirt felt uncomfortable—badly prepared for the occasion.

"Your grandfather, Valentine Bertolow, has been supporting you with a small trust fund which was intended to just suffice without luxuries."

Although there had been only two of them, Martin could well remember how money had always been an issue. His mother, a small spare woman full of determination had had to work hard for it. Martin's summer work supplemented their supply. Some meager funds came from some mysterious source from his deceased father's family. What it added hardly sufficed, although later, by design, it had provided for his education at an Ivy League college.

The interview was being held in an ample office where the solid, dark, old fashioned furniture contrasted with the imposing ultramodern skyscraper in which it was located. The window looked out on other skyscrapers, and if one bothered to look down, Martin imagined, the bustling of the city, strangely absent in the seclusion of the office. Martin could discern the far away shining blue presence of Lake Michigan. The walls were cream-colored. On one wall, a Winslow Homer painting of a sea scene seemed completely at home in the office's environment.

"However," Mr. Cyril Appleton continued, "he left you in his will another trust fund for when you reached maturity, in his mind at the age of twenty-five, your present age. You must have know about it, although you were never told exactly what it represented. That fund has been well invested and after taxes has reached the level of fifteen million, give or take a million. In his instructions at the time of his death, he expressed a preference for leaving it in the trust, but you have access to the capital as well if you so wish. Bear in mind that the investments have proven lucrative. We can discuss the details at a later date after the will is officially filed."

Martin swallowed hard. His vocal cords seemed to have become paralyzed. "Mm! Mm!" he said.

"Perhaps I should explain some of the background." Appleton continued, "Your grandfather, Mr. Bertolow, as you might know was a Holocaust survivor and very eccentric, although I do not presume to pass judgement on such matters. His original name was Jacob Berenstein. He built a fortune on very clever real estate investments. The disappointment of his life was that his only son, your father, married outside his faith. When your father died, your grandfather was emotionally unable to maintain ties with his daughter-in-law and child, a situation he strongly regretted later on in life, although by then his health had faltered." After a long pause, the lawyer spoke again. "Anyway, let us know what you wish us to do. In the meantime, I have taken the liberty of starting a checking account under your name for two hundred thousand to take care of any immediate needs. You'll have to sign the cards and I will be glad to forward them to the bank." The lawyer, handed him two cards and a checkbook.

As Martin signed the cards, Appleton smiled for the first time. A tight surprisingly shy smile. "It's none of my business, but what do you think you'll do as soon as you cash some of that money?"

Martin was completely confused although he hoped he'd covered his shock. "Oh, I'll probably get my dry-cleaning out of hock!"

Appleton laughed, a dry contained laugh. "Well, don't advertise your fortune or you'll have more headaches than you can handle. It's bad enough for us mortals. There are more leeches, salesmen and crooks in this world than you can shake a stick at." The laugh had now turned into an improbable chuckle.

More than ever, the secret of success, Martin thought, was to go slowly until able to see the whole picture. More from need than inclination—jobs were scarce and mostly boring—he had been working as a waiter at the *Black Orchid*, an upscale restaurant which knew the value of *croissettes* and good wines. No reason to change at least for now. The work was mostly pleasant although at times on weekends it could become demanding, requiring speed along with cheerfulness and efficiency. The tips were generally generous and in the past he had depended on them. At this point, of course, they had become more a measure of approval than an actual necessity. What appealed to him most were the customers and the intriguing bits of conversation that would set his imagination along pathways that were probably far from reality. It was a world he had never known. Sometimes, when a bottle or two of wine had been ordered, the job of keeping the glasses full would bring him back to snatches of conversation that could actually tell a story. He had been intrigued by a rather attractive young woman. She was probably younger than the middle twenties she seemed to project. Small-breasted, her cleavage was revealed more modestly than presently fashionable. Her light brown hair was coiffed to perfection—the kind of look that appeared casual but in fact represented the skill of an expensive professional. She had a graceful way of moving and an attractive expression even when she pouted, as she was doing at that moment. Her words didn't need any intricate interpretation. "The only sane plan for a woman is to marry for money … making your own is too hard. By the time you're comfy, you'd be an old woman. Of course if you inherit it's even better. Who needs a man to go along with the money if you can help it?"

Martin's smile was entirely internal but his thoughts contained some regret. He'd taken a quick, guarded look at the three women and found the other two were attractive as well. One was older, dark-haired and much amused. The other a blonde, dressed elegantly in a black dress. Nobody ever notices a waiter unless he has some unusual feature, such a dark moustache, a big mole or birthmark on his face. In his case, Martin knew that he might as well be invisible. He knew that in all likelihood as a waiter he'd never have the opportunity to sample the goods, so to speak Perhaps, he thought, if he were to travel in the world at large he might be able to get involved with attractive women. He filled the wine glasses and went on to the counter to check what order had been readied. The chef took pride in the food never standing around for too long. A hot blooded voluble Frenchman, he didn't take failures of the serving staff lightly. The temperature of the dish was as important as the balance of the spicing, and Martin concurred.

Visiting his mother, Patricia Bertolow, Martin had revealed his good fortune but she didn't want to hear the details. "Don't tell me. I don't want to know. It's good enough to know the old son of a bitch came through. I knew about a trust fund but I thought it was as mean-spirited as the man himself and the previous one."

Martin had long recognized the effort to ignore facts as a facet of his mother's personality. He thought of it as the ostrich syndrome. But it was too much imbedded in her makeup to be challenged. Besides he appreciated the devoted role she always had played in his life.

"No, Mom. This one is very generous. The first thing we have to do is to get you out of this apartment into something more substantial."

The efficiency apartment included one room, kitchen and bathroom. It was furnished sparsely with scuffed pieces that he remembered from his childhood. As he recalled, his mother had re-upholstered the couch herself. A daunting task that had left some folds of cloth where they didn't belong.

"No need for that at all. My friends are around here."

"Well, we can find something around here, I'm sure."

Although he was beginning to feel the need to widen his horizons, the idea of changing his lifestyle hadn't gelled in his mind. He knew only too well that the world was big and he had examined only a minute portion of it. In addition, his experience with women was quite limited. Aside from watching attractive women at a distance, he had had almost no experience at all. The exception of course was Nancy.

Nancy worked as a waitress at the *Black Orchid*. Martin had always considered her a fellow worker and nothing more. She was not unattractive. Her stringy brown hair was held in a bun. Her breasts were prominent. Driving her home on a rainy day, she had asked him to please come in. He was rewarded by an opened-mouth kiss—her body tightly clinging to him. He later regretted following her initiative, and although the sex that followed had been pleasant and interesting, from then on he had had difficulty in keeping his distance from her. He should have shown more self-control. The role he was forced to play must have hurt her feelings and yet he knew that if he actually took up with her, she would be hurt even more.

Getting away from Nancy and the world he knew had an unexpected source of help.

At a table in the *Black Orchid*, two men were talking earnestly after ordering wine and their food. "That trip on Merv's yacht is going to be a scream. Imagine a cruise through the Great Lakes and the *Marie Antoinette* is more of a liner than a yacht!" One of the two said, "I fully expect to get laid nightly." The man was tall and handsome, and as he sipped his expensive *Beauremond* wine something about him announced that he thought he was God's gift to women. His expression was rather unattractive to Martin, but then he wasn't a woman. The other man was blond and red-faced, almost brick colored, as if he was flushed but Martin suspected that was his natural color. He had to attend another table but heard some more of the conversation later. The second man was talking.

"You can boast all you want but I'll bet you'll never be able to get into Laura. She's after big game."

"I'll bet you one big one!"

"Don't be stupid. I'd have to take your word for it and you know what I think of your word. You were cheating even at Monopoly when you were a child and I don't think you have changed much except for your oversized libido."

"Do you know who has been invited? Maybe Laura won't even be there. Merv makes such a secret out of everything!"

"Hardly a secret if you know where to look."

"Yeah? You know where to look?"

"Why, the list is next door, where the grand vizier of the *Orchid* is now organizing the spread. Merv always uses the *Orchid's* kitchen staff and in fact its nucleus will be on the ship."

"You're kidding!"

Martin had to move on, the headwaiter had already directed a very disapproving look in this direction. But then Martin didn't need any more information. His sense of adventure had taken over. As he well knew, *Sun Tzu* in *The Art of War* says "One who is prepared and waits for the unprepared will be victorious."

To his surprise when he was finally able to insert himself in the mystery room, there was no such list. But he saw a lab top computer sitting on the desk. However, no list appeared when he activated the computer or the word processing software. Fiddling with it nervously, he tried out a few possible passwords to get to the hidden files. They might do just as well without a password since the magic word was the name of the ship, "Marie Antoinette." It wasn't difficult to insert his name and address on the list which was in alphabetical order. He imagined the roster was for the purpose of sending out invitations and for place names at the tables.

It didn't occur to him until later that his ploy had its dangers. Hopefully, the ship's kitchen staff from the *Black Orchid* wouldn't have any contact with the guests.

A few days later Martin received an invitation in the mail. On the day the guests were welcomed aboard he went to the ship with some trepidation. As he had overheard, it really was more like a liner than a yacht. He already knew that

Merv could afford its use despite his youth because it actually belonged to his father who also was responsible for the upkeep. Martin had to relinquish his suitcase to the cart provided and scrawled his name on a card. What to bring with him had caused him some anxiety. Should he favor the formal or the informal. His compromise was to carry a little bit of both.

"Sir," he was told on arrival, "the luggage will be delivered to your cabin." At the gangplank a man in a white sailing uniform checked his name on the list he held and let him through. At the top an attractive woman asked for his name and entrusted him with a sheet giving him the assigned cabin number and dining room table.

"Breakfast will be served until shortly before lunchtime if you wish. Then we'll sail," she informed him.

As he was walking through the corridors to find his cabin he wondered whether he was dressed properly. He had assumed informal attire, t-shirt and cotton pants would be sufficient at least for the first day. One of his recurrent worries had been whether he would be dressed properly for the occasion and whether he had assumed the right amount of informality and *joie de vivre*. He was in a milieu entirely new for him. Was he going to stand out like a sore thumb? He was reassured to see the other young people coursing the corridors had much the same idea and were all dressed informally. Some men and women were actually in shorts. After that he stopped worrying. Why should he care anyway? You can be a hit by being much like everybody else or being entirely eccentric.

After admiring his cabin, small but efficiently laid out, he made his way to the dining room to have breakfast. His encounters with his fellow passengers required only a polite smile on passing. However, when he arrived at his destination he found a woman sitting across at his assigned table. The dining room was relatively small; there were only five tables, each set up for four persons. Only two others were occupied.

"I'm Martin Bertolow," he said introducing himself standing across from her. The introduction was entirely superfluous since his name was printed very conspicuously on a card at his place.

"I'm Laura … Laura Duran." With a smile, she shook his hand without getting up.

Suddenly alert, he realized that she was the woman he had admired at the *Black Orchid* and who had voiced the need to marry for money. Of course, she didn't show any signs of recognition. As he had always suspected, as a waiter he had been totally unnoticed. She turned out to be very friendly. Face to face, she looked even more attractive than she had before and much younger.

Was she the Laura the two playboys were betting on? He hoped not.

"My God, Martin! I'm totally intimidated! All these important and rich people! I'm impressed and I have no clue about how I should dress or behave even though I have known some of them for a long time! But things are different after you reach a certain age. You look normal. Perhaps I can hang around with you."

Martin smiled shyly. Her attitude, much like his own, was a surprise. "I'd be delighted." And then, "But do I really look that harmless? A Milquetoast?"

"Harmless, meaning not threatening … kind … friendly."

"That's better."

"What do you do for a living, may I ask?"

"This and that. Right now I'm on a cruise trying to enjoy myself."

"You must be marking time right after college, like I'm doing."

"Well, not exactly, there isn't much you can do with a Master's in history."

"Better than being rich as Croesus and doing nothing like half of this crowd. Anyway, I'm glad I met you. You seem normal! And friendly!"

"I'm glad I passed the test. I hope this is just a preliminary evaluation and we'll have time to get to know each other better."

Martin was amazed at how daring he seemed to be on automatic pilot.

"One way or another we'll get to know each other. There aren't that many people in the group. Most Mervin's friends. They can be a pain. Many of the unaccompanied men are on the make with completely predictable lines. Promise to save me from them if something like that happens. I can't stand boring men on the make. I'll touch my nose and please come to my rescue immediately!"

"Ooh! Just like in baseball! Secret signals from the catcher! But wouldn't it be simpler to tell them to go to hell?"

"My dear Martin, you have yet to discover that I'm a total coward under all my bluster. Some of the guests I have known all my life. Other men are socially prominent, although I don't know why I care. I guess I'm still not entirely grown up."

"So, why did you accept the invitation to the cruise?"

"Oh, who knows. Curiosity. I have known Mervin forever. I even dated him once or twice when in college. I certainly don't want to renew our connection but I was curious. Curiosity might have killed the cat but it certainly tantalizes."

A woman in a fashionable tennis outfit approached the table. Laura addressed her, "Hello, Glenn."

She sat down at their table. "Hi there! I really should skip breakfast. Lunch is going to start soon and I can't afford another calorie. Too bad I can't resist the lure of pastry and coffee."

"Glenn, meet a friend of mine, Martin Bertolow."

And so it went throughout the days that followed. He stayed with her whenever he could and discovered she seemed to enjoy his company.

Martin didn't find too many compatible souls with a few exceptions. Mark was an African-American.

"I'm the token," he quipped. Martin couldn't resist taking the bait knowing that it was a trap.

"Token black?" he asked.

"No, no, no!" countered Mark. "Token normal."

"Come on Mark, there must be other exceptions such as Laura."

"Mm!Mm! I guess Laura is another token!" But he wouldn't explain farther and continued on the same vein. "You see my parents are both physicians and together they only clear half a mil per year. I owe being invited to my father's relieving Mervin of his burst appendix."

There were a number of attractive young women but Martin felt none matched Laura's irrepressible earnestness and openness. The men were another matter. They were all smooth, well-spoken and handsomer than him. One of them, Gaston, was particularly oily and he couldn't understand why Laura tolerated his presence. At times, when these men approached Laura he'd felt a surprising stab of jealousy. For goodness sake, he had just met the woman, he thought. What was cooking inside his brain was probably just part of the primeval impulses that young men and particularly foolish ones have. But later he decided he really cared for her.

The five days on the ship were packed with significance. Laura was his entry into a world he hadn't known. She always introduced him as a dear friend. How far was that from boyfriend? Was it meaningless like most of the relationship he saw within the social set on the ship? On top of that he felt that he was always about to be identified as an intruder either by his behavior or realization that he couldn't possibly be a friend of Mervin. The supreme test came when alone he had found himself facing Mervin, whose picture he had seen before. Mervin just smiled and said, "Oh, how are you … ehm … Martin?" Somebody must have told him the names of the guests he couldn't remember having met before.

The continuous parties, the games, the dancing and flirting were not unpleasant but he was glad when the trip was over.

Eventually the time came when Laura and Martin had to part. He felt uneasy and wished it didn't have to happen. He kissed her lightly. "Will it be okay to call on you?"

She laughed her full amused laugh. "You mean, will I date you?"

He nodded.

"Why don't you say so? You're really something!"

"Something good or bad?"

"Something."

She kissed him almost fiercely. "If you don't call I'll have to call you." After a pause, "Did I make you jealous, you know, with Gaston. Part of it was that I couldn't avoid him gracefully, part of it was that I wanted to shake you up a little. You're such a lump! Half of the time I didn't even know whether you cared for me! I promise I'll never try to make you jealous again."

"I do care for you!"

"Good! That makes two of us on the same wavelength. I care for you. If you were at all observant you would have understood that!"

What happens between a man and a woman is always unpredictable. The fact is that after that they saw each other almost every day. There was the day when they were both partially disrobed, holding each other tight. Their breathing had accelerated and Martin while holding her was almost overcome with desire.

"Laura," he said putting into words what was troubling him. "I want you very badly. But I don't want just a roll in the hay. It might be selfish of me but I want you on a permanent basis."

"Oh, Martin you're so silly. You think that I just want a roll in the hay? You underestimate my possessiveness. I wouldn't want one without the other. And you can say it in words. Men are so peculiar! You love me, don't you?"

"Yes, yes, yes."

"Well, I spared you saying the inevitable. You owe me."

There was no time for teasing or conversation after that. The sex first tentative and always tender became passionate.

Martin really meant what he had said; he realized that he couldn't do without her.

He laughed off her comment he'd overheard when she was at the *Black Orchid*. Marrying for money certainly wasn't on her mind. But eventually, he teased her about it.

"I heard once that you thought a woman should marry for money."

Laura laughed. "Where could you possibly have heard that? Yes indeed. I've said it many times. I've also said that a woman shouldn't marry if it can be avoided. That's a hook. It makes for great conversations. The ones that deny the wiseness of that course most strongly are the ones that think that way. Very interesting, or amusing, or both!"

The idea of getting married seemed to have developed slowly all by itself. But in their intimate conversations it seemed to be assumed. She finally said it, "Are you going to talk about it or do you want to keep it hidden."

He knew exactly what she meant and that's when they made firm plans.

Laura thought he should meet her grandmother. Laura and her sister, Jill, had been raised primarily by her grandmother, Louise. Their parents had died when the sisters were little in an unfortunate car accident. As he understood it, they both owed their grandmother a good deal and her opinion mattered to Laura. That was one of the reasons she had arranged the visit for Martin to meet her.

After the customary greetings, Jill, a college student, excused herself—something about an exam she was preparing for.

Martin had felt that from the moment he had met Grandma she had been discreetly scrutinizing him and then had found an excuse to be alone with him. He didn't mind. In her shoes he would have felt compelled to probe. Laura was as precious to him as she must be to her grandmother.

Laura's grandmother peered over her spectacles at Martin. "I understand you two intend to get married." Her eyes which had shown amusement and interest when exchanging pleasantries, were at that moment riveted on his and severe like those of a schoolteacher when Martin as a young boy hadn't quite behaved.

He hadn't expected the veiled antagonism. "That's our present plan," he answered.

"I thought marriage was no longer fashionable. And aren't you two too young to consider such a binding commitment?"

"We both have been out of college for a while. We both know what we feel—what I believe is a deep and enduring love."

"You have a college degree in history I was told. I believe you told Laura that you have been working as a waiter."

"That is indeed true."

"You must understand that I don't feel your prospects are very promising. Besides, how would we know that you're not a fortune hunter?"

Her attitude came as a surprise. Martin laughed. "I'm quite able to make a living. And is there a fortune to hunt?"

"Don't pretend ignorance. You know that Laura and Jill will be inheriting a good deal of money when my husband dies and he has been ill for some time."

"I'm afraid you're on the wrong track. I never bothered to find out what Laura's economic status was. True, I saw she hung around with the wealthy but that's all. Don't you have any respect for your granddaughter's good sense and perspicacity?"

Grandma laughed. "You'd be surprised how silly a girl can be when she's in love."

"I think silly is the last word I would use to describe your granddaughter. You've made an outstanding job of raising her. Well, she's the one that will have to decide. You can bring up your suspicions to her. I promise that I won't hold it against you."

"Rather presumptuous of you, isn't it? You didn't convince me and I'm not sure I like you."

Laura, who certainly must have understood the subterfuge that had sent her scurrying to the kitchen, reentered with tea and cookies. She studiously placed the tray in front of them. Each cup and small plate was placed where each of them would be sitting.

"Ooh! So serious!"

"Well, your grandmother has reservations about our impending marriage. I'm sure she has discussed it with you."

"Grandma is very protective of us. She's always been."

Martin couldn't disagree. "I commend her for that. You two are well worth protecting!"

Grandma objected. "Oh, Laura you're exaggerating. True, I'm concerned about your welfare but you make it sound as if I worry all the time."

"You do worry all the time and it's so silly."

"Whoa!" Grandma laughed "Nobody realized you were that Bertolow. Were you trying to make me feel foolish?"

"Oh Grandma, you shouldn't have been so foolish. You can tell Martin is a great guy, just the kind of man for me."

But Martin was serious. "Not at all. I just like to be judged for myself. Besides, I had hardly got accustomed to being the recipient of all that money.

Leave the lucre out of your thoughts. Don't you feel better now that you have scrutinized me thoroughly so that you know I'm okay and we both are mature enough to marry and love each other?"

INTERMEZZO

Lucy had come to the engagement party at Noreen's urging, the argument being that the two of them hadn't seen each other for ages and the party was for all intents and purposes an open house given by the parents of the future bride. Although Noreen was acquainted with the family, Lucy didn't know them or the betrothed at all. In a way, their taking advantage of the hospitality was tacky but then most people do things like that at one time or another.

Lucy and Noreen had been girlfriends since forever, but at the party Lucy must have offended her as Noreen had walked off in a huff. Lucy was trying to figure out what Noreen had found so offensive and whether she was likely to reappear. From what Lucy could reconstruct, it had something to do with her comment that Noreen had a propensity to attach herself to totally unsuitable men. As if Lucy was one to criticize! Her divorce from Jeff Boyton had been public and spectacular. After the fact, her exaggerated accusations had embarrassed her, although she had clung to them to maintain a pretense of dignity. How could she have been so vindictive, so petty! Jeff had been an unmitigated prig and a bore, but he hadn't been unfaithful and hadn't stolen money from his corporation. The accusations in the newspaper accounts turned out to be untrue. One of the partners had been guilty of the larceny. Although exonerated, Jeff's career had been ruined. A woman had set her sights on Jeff, but as far as Lucy could tell the interloper had been unsuccessful. None of that changed the fact that Jeff was too much infatuated with his own opinions and had no respect for hers. After the breakup she decided that they had gotten hitched when they were too young to think through the implications in their lives.

Lucy found herself sitting on a sofa with her back to several middle-aged women. They spoke animatedly and then laughed. Despite the talk behind her, she could hear background chatter from the adjoining room as well as music.

Not interested in mere gossip, she was making every effort not to listen. She nursed her drink trying to decide what to do.

She didn't know why the voice from the group behind her finally broke through her musings. The merriment had been supplanted by a more sober tone.

"You can imagine my distress with my daughter, Claire. Like her previous engagement—this new boyfriend, Jeff Boyton, will be a complete bust. Totally unsuitable. A criminal background—he swindled the company he was working for. Has been divorced and is incapable of taking responsibility. He's probably cheating on Claire already! You can't imagine how painful it is for me. And she's talking about a June wedding!"

A soothing voice tried to console her.

Lucy turned and took a good look at the woman responsible for the lamentations. She could only see her profile. Poor Jeff! She hoped the happy couple would learn to ignore the mother-in-law that came with Claire.

She returned to the adjoining room and grabbed a Manhattan at the bar. She turned down an invitation to dance. She just wasn't in the mood. Why did some men look so young? Or had she really gotten so old? She saw Noreen, who seemed to be ready to leave. She hastened to intercept her before she reached the door. Lucy had to make amends. Noreen meant too much to her.

"Noreen! My apologies. I spoke like a jerk. Besides what you do is your business!"

"You know when you confide in your best friend you expect some sympathy—some understanding."

"Sorry sweetie, I must be in a terrible mood. I'll do better another time."

She was rewarded by a smile which tried very hard to be a smirk of disapproval. But Lucy knew that everything would be alright.

"I'll call you soon."

They waved at each other and Noreen was gone. Lucy would really try to be more diplomatic without lying, she promised herself. She was sure she could do it with some effort.

As she turned, she found herself facing the woman who had been talking about Jeff in such a censorious tone. Lucy couldn't help herself.

"You know Jeff Boyton is not a thief and his divorce was not his fault."

The woman glanced at a companion beside her and then turned toward Lucy with ice in her eyes. "Who might you be? And why can't you mind your own business."

Lucy felt herself blushing. "I couldn't help hearing you. You were rather loud. And I ought to know about Jeff. I'm his ex."

"Well, well. One more strike against him as marriage material. An ex-wife who's still in love with him!" And she walked away with only contempt on her face.

Lucy was shaken. The old bitch! She certainly knew how to hit where it hurt, even though Lucy was certain there wasn't an iota of truth in what the old biddy had just said—Lucy had just stopped being petty and facing the world with a chip on her shoulder.

Weeks later, leafing through the wedding announcements, she was pleased to find out that the old bitch hadn't succeeded in discouraging Claire's and Jeff's engagement. There was even a photograph of the happy pair, Claire smiling and Jeff trying to show what a serious man he was. Claire was definitely very pretty. Absurdly, for a moment Lucy felt a stab of jealousy. No woman should look that perfect. But then Claire would have to put up with her groom. Jeff hadn't changed much. Lucy only felt good-natured affection for him. He wasn't such a bad guy. She was glad that he had successfully emerged from his crisis as she herself had. She hoped that he had matured some since the two of them had divorced. She knew that she had. Putting the newspaper down she realized that a cloud had lifted from her. A chapter in her life had closed and she was ready for her future.

ICE AND FIRE

For some time Josh had dated Amanda who worked in Personnel, or in today's duplicitous parlance, "Human Resources". He had been taken with Amanda. Attractive and perky with light brown hair and twinkle in her sepia-colored eyes, she had charmed him. She tended to be too frank, however. When breaking up with him, she had told him that despite liking him a lot, she had found him irresponsible, self-centered and immature. Insulted and hurt he still thought about her often and in the depths of his soul knew she was right. Although he would have denied it, he regretted the outcome. Somehow, he was left rather emotionally vulnerable.

Whether his vulnerability or his immaturity was responsible for the later chapter in his life, he couldn't tell. From the first time he had seen Mrs. Insell, Josh had dubbed her the "Ice Maiden." He had heard her called Maura. He first saw her at a party for the top executives of Moulten International, although she didn't stay long. Their exchange of a few words was very unsatisfactory. He had wished to make an impression—a beautiful woman, perfectly proportioned, dressed in the latest fashions. Her well-coiffed dark blonde hair looked as if it were in a careless but probably expensive arrangement. With few and impersonal words, she'd kept her distance. Considerably older than him, possibly in her middle thirties, she had the allure of a mature woman. As the boss's wife she offered another attraction. In his twenty-five years, Josh had dated several women but had rarely been so strongly captivated.

He didn't seen Maura again until the group's Christmas Party. Louis Insell, her husband, had stayed only briefly. Impeccably dressed, he was some years older than his wife—a vigorous late forties or early fifties. Josh couldn't help noticing the diamond ring he wore or his very expensive Italian shoes, Marimondo no less—a mark of vanity. The shoes must have set him back by six to eight hundred dollars.

Josh didn't understand why the man bothered with such conventional social efforts or rented a special hall to entertain the populace. Reputed to be a bastard, his most favored ploy was to fire any employee who reached a certain high salary because of seniority. He also enjoyed berating recent additions to the staff for its entertainment value. Apparently, on this occasion he had to leave town on an urgent personal matter. Maura stayed a little longer and smiled and chatted briefly with many and then she headed for the door. In the hall, there were many lights, appropriate Christmas and winter decorations, music and a dance floor. The group of musicians was small but accomplished. Although the party had just begun, some couples had started dancing to old-fashioned music that required slow, sensuous movements, not the more frequent frenetic dances of the day. Josh felt once more he was missing an opportunity. He intercepted her and actually dared to ask Maura to dance. She looked up in surprise and with a guarded smile assented.

Josh knew he was a good dancer and so was she. When they were near the middle of the piece, he pulled her close to him in a very intimate embrace. He found his contact with her exciting. She moved with him without comment, but then murmured, "Not here you fool. Wait for me at my car, a blue Porsche," and pushed him to a less revealing distance.

At the end of the piece, Josh left. He thought for sure he wouldn't be able to find her car among the many in the poorly illuminated parking lot and that she might be just playing with him. Perhaps his daring would cost him his job. He felt better when he found the car. Maura kept him waiting for at least ten minutes. Josh excited and yet cautious was impatient. When she unlocked the car and sat on the driver's seat he joined her on the passenger side. The car hummed alive and from then on he didn't know what was happening or how to proceed.

In her luxurious house he felt like a little boy visiting an exalted and strict older relative. He didn't know what to do or what to say. In her eyes, he thought he must appear to be a bumbling immature fool. The obviously expensive furniture and luxury were also intimidating. There were even some modern paintings which might have been originals, to Josh reminiscent of Kandinsky. The offered drink was accepted and only delayed matters. Then fortunately she took the initiative.

"Aren't you going to kiss me?" she murmured.

On the couch, her facile hands and mouth seemed to touch him everywhere. Their clothes came off quickly. That's when she started teasing him, once embracing him, once pushing him aside. Finally, they were together in motion until he exploded inside her.

He was with her many times after their first encounter, but didn't get to know her any better. It was like being on fire; he wasn't in love with her, didn't love her, yet he would have found it hard to give her up.

He had heard it said before that "sex isn't everything"—a saying he'd accepted with unspoken skepticism. With time he began to understand what it meant. He found himself missing Amanda's easy comradery. Josh guessed Maura had a busy social life and many friends. She must have had opinions, likes, dislikes, hopes, plans for the future. Yet Josh knew nothing of those. Any attempt on his part to lead their conversations to any of those directions was quickly deflected. After a few desultory questions, she didn't seem to be interested in his life. To his surprise he found himself growing less eager for his encounters with Maura. Eventually, considering the risk it seemed wiser to break up the affair, a course he decided to follow with some trepidation. In all his previous experiences, the superficial relationships had either faded spontaneously or had been broken up by the woman.

They were to spend time together in a hotel out of town. That is the time to broach a breakup, he thought. As they got out of the Porsche the impossible happened. Two men with masks appeared between the cars. One seized Maura. With a surge of anger, Josh responded instinctively and hit the man hard with his right fist. But it was over for him very quickly. He learned later that the second man had shot him.

Feeling very weak, Josh was conscious of a silence broken by swishing noises and occasionally soft voices. The smells were definitely medicinal. Then he was being conveyed elsewhere and strong hands transferred him to another bed. He surmised he was in a hospital. A television set controlled by his roommate who was separated from him by a thick curtain was a continual disturbance. But then he was transferred again, this time to a private room. He recognized the presence of his mother, sobbing. This, he thought, might signify a worsening of his state. But then he remembered that she always cried at any crisis, large or small. He wasn't immediately conscious of his mother being replaced by Detective Molino and a male companion, Sargent Ellmart. Evelyn Molino was a woman with a severe appearance sometimes broken unexpectedly by a smile. Her nose was straight and her dark hair was pulled back. Dressed in a business suit, she looked more like a secretary than a policewoman. The man accompanying her was a nondescript short man with sandy hair and wearing glasses.

Molino ignored Josh's state of confusion and made light conversation. What college did he graduate from? What did he do at work? Where did he usually vacation? Then she focused on the events she was interested in. Josh wasn't quite sure what she was saying. He still felt woozy and had difficulty in focusing until he heard that Maura had been kidnapped. What did he remember? Josh gathered his wits. But his information wasn't very useful. Although apparently a mask had been displaced by his blow and found bloody in the parking lot, he hadn't seen the face. Molino seemed to know what he and Maura were doing there, but didn't press the point. Who else knew where and when they were going? Had he noticed somebody following them? The answer to both questions was negative. Molino explained some of the possible indications of a clandestine surveillance. But Josh couldn't help her.

As time went by, Josh realized that the news media had not covered the event in any detail. They had not mentioned the kidnapping, probably a silence imposed by the police for the victim's safety.

It didn't take long for a few of the guys and gals of Moulten to come visiting him in the hospital, although he was recovering quickly. The bullets hadn't lodged anywhere vital and they had been removed surgically. He hoped the crowd of coworkers didn't know about his interlude with Maura. He wasn't ashamed of what had happened, but he wasn't proud of it either, and certainly a rumor of that magnitude could cost him his job. His visitors brought a good deal of meaningless chatter, flowers, chocolate and balloons, some with indecent humorous imprints. Although he had no close friends in the group, he appreciated their demonstration of comradery.

Toward the end of their brief visit, Amanda made an appearance. At first she surveyed the room shyly and smiled at him. His heart lurched into an unexpected rhythm. Did he still have a chance with her? He had been an immature idiot but perhaps she hadn't judged him too harshly. When she approached him, he grasped her hand.

"Can you please stay for a little while?"

She stayed after the others had left and again he held her hand. He realized that she meant everything to him.

"You were absolutely right about me. I'm a hopeless fool. A lot has happened lately and I have learned a lot. I can't talk about it now, but would you consider seeing me again?"

"It all depends. But first let me ask you something. There is gossip that you were having an affair with Maura Insell. Is there any truth to that?"

Josh blushed and felt himself tightening. He wasn't going to keep it a secret from Amanda, but he had planned on telling her a lot later. Could this signal the end of all his hopes? He wanted to tell her about how much he regretted it. That it was over. But he just couldn't put the words together.

"Yes," is all he could say.

"Well," she said, "we'll talk about these things after you're out of here." She squeezed his hand and left.

After leaving the hospital, Josh still felt weak and dizzy. His mother's fretting over him and showing up at his apartment every morning didn't make matters easier. She had advice on how he could recover his strength and frequently brought him something to eat. She never realized what was tormenting him.

In addition to his uncertainty about his friendship with Amanda, Josh couldn't let his mind rest about Maura's fate. After all, he had been partially responsible for her quandary. Molino came to discuss matters with him and didn't give the warning that he should keep off the case. In innumerable mysteries Josh had read that was always the attitude of the police. Molino was even of the opinion that something Josh knew might be the key to breaking the case.

"Is the husband going to come up with the money?" Josh asked.

"It would seem to be a good idea to go ahead so that we could trace the money when the ransom is picked up by the kidnappers, but Insell doesn't seem interested. I would guess that his attitude is "let the bitch fry." He seems to know what she was doing when they seized her and he isn't the forgiving kind."

"It sounds stupid but I feel in part responsible. I'm not exactly an angel but if I can be of help, I'll do the best I can."

Without even having been with him, Amanda had become very important to Josh. It was as if he had reexamined all his values and emotions. What he felt for her if not love was something close to it. He felt compelled to meet with her and explain. They met at the café they used to go to when still dating. After his account of what had taken place, she voiced her misgivings.

"You sure behaved stupidly. Still, I don't understand what you're trying to tell me. You want to be with me, but you're continuing your involvement with that woman."

"It's not an involvement in the usual sense. I feel responsible for what happened. She is a human being and if events follow their normal course she might die. Perhaps it was just a meaningless affair but I was there as her companion and unable to do anything. It's very upsetting. It's a question of accepting my responsibility."

"Boy! You sure can dish out a lot of horseshit!"

A long silence followed and Josh was slowly giving up hope.

"Does that mean that you want me to get lost?"

"Now you're being childish again. Why should I want you to get lost? What I want is to be included in everything that happens! It sounds interesting." She laughed and then continued, "And you might do something stupid that will put you in danger unless I'm there to counsel you! Like getting involved with that old bitch again."

Molino was of a totally different mind from what she had implied in her conversation with Josh previously. She berated him for discussing the case with Amanda. Hadn't she requested discretion? Josh knew that she hadn't. He figured the policewoman planned to manipulate him in some way. Regardless of what was said or what she wanted, she had to face a *fait accompli*. Amanda was there with her two hundred watt amused smile. What was Molino supposed to do, arrest them?

Given the lack of clues there were only three possible ways to proceed. One way was finding out how the villains knew the site and time of Maura's and Josh's meeting. Josh suggested an obvious alternative: they could fake the paying of ransom and follow the shipment. Another possibility would be to plant false information with the media to give the impression that Josh had seen the face of the criminal he had unmasked and they were in the process of completing composite drawings. Then Josh could serve as bait for a trap.

Amanda was totally against using Josh as bait. "Both of you must be out of your minds!"

"Let's fake a payment," Molino volunteered. "Counterfeit currency we seized in a raid can be used, with permission from the feds, of course." However, the ploy would put the victim in danger unless they moved very fast.

After a few days, a request for ransom was received by Insell. He communicated the demand to the police, although Molino already knew about it from the tap on Insell's phone.

Over Amanda's strong objections Josh volunteered to carry the loot.

Molino laughed. "How could I possibly use a civilian. It could cost me my job!"

Josh responded, "First you want my help, then you don't. You know that they demanded the delivery not involve the police. I don't know whether one of your undercover persons would do, but the kidnappers certainly would know that I'm not police. They saw me well enough when they grabbed Mrs. Insell."

"Well … maybe. It may sound dangerous but we'll be watching. Usually they give instructions which they keep changing so that the ransom has to be moved constantly until they finally grab it. That's the way most kidnappers make sure that there is nobody following." After a short interruption she continued, "I'm sure we can handle it. I will have enough people. It's a question of moving our forces every time they change the location of the delivery. Very difficult, but it can be done. Then we would follow discreetly whomever picked up the loot. Supposedly upon receipt of the money, they'll tell Insell where his wife has been dropped."

Amanda was still objecting. "Absolutely not. It's an unacceptable level of danger."

"Amanda, you know how I feel about it. Please let me do it."

Amanda looked determined, an expression that in Josh's thoughts didn't take away any of her attractiveness.

"I'm not sure she deserves your taking the risk."

"It's not a question of deserving. As far as I'm concerned it's a question of accepting responsibility … what I should be doing."

"Would you not go if I asked you not to?"

"Yes."

"Are you really not in love with that bitch."

"Amanda, I love you. Period."

This was the first time he had made an unequivocal statement and it seemed to have the desired effect. She ceased to object but it was clear that she didn't care for the plan which unduly exposed Josh.

The day arrived when Insell was given instructions. The ransom had to be taken to a 7-Eleven convenience store by one man, not a policeman. If he was followed or if he was armed, the deal would be off. If they were satisfied that their conditions were being met, the pay phone would ring and more instructions would follow.

Amanda spoke out, "If you go I want you to wear body armor of the latest design."

Molino didn't object and a jacket was provided. Once he put it on, Josh wondered whether he wanted to wear it. It felt uncomfortable and confining, but then he had promised Amanda.

The night came. It seemed to arrive sooner than expected. Josh who had felt he could complete the delivery easily suddenly felt terrified. His mouth had suddenly turned dry and his heart was drumming. The bag containing the fake loot was in the trunk of his car. He was worried about his own safety and Maura's life if the job was botched. For some reason as he drove to his destination, the night seemed darker than it had ever been. The lighted signs of the various businesses lining the streets and avenues were confusing. He almost passed the well-illuminated store and had to brake suddenly. Fortunately there was almost no traffic, although a car or two had passed him from the opposite direction.

Upon entering the 7-Eleven, he waved at the employee who quickly ceased to watch him. Then leaning against the wall, Josh watched the pay phone, waiting for the phone to ring. He had been a few minutes earlier than the 11 pm of his instructions. His wait was not unlike that for the proverbial watched pot which never boils. He might have done better if he had been alert to movements in the store. A masked man suddenly appeared in front of him. Josh's first thought was it was just his luck to witness a holdup. What happened was totally unexpected. The explosion of the gun in the man's hand caused Josh to fall to the floor, against the wall. The pain in his chest was considerable. The man disappeared as quickly as he had appeared. A police cruiser arrived almost immediately. Josh wasn't incapacitated and moving didn't seem to be hard or painful aside from what he would have expected from a sports injury. Despite his dazed condition, since the shooter had not gone to the counter or attempted to collect cash, Josh realized after a few seconds that he had been the target and that the bullet-proof jacket must have done its job.

The telephone started ringing and Josh afraid of being interrupted by the policemen, yelled. "I'm okay. Let me take the call."

The two policemen must have been following Molino's instructions because they ignored Josh and went to interview the frightened employee that was hiding behind the counter.

Josh seized the phone. A gravelly voice instructed him to take himself to the Watercress Shopping Center leaving the bag with the money in the trunk of his car.

It took him a few seconds to start the car. His hand holding the car key was trembling. He was terrified. The thought occurred to him that a third party had entered the game. Killing him was certainly not to the kidnappers' advantage.

Molino had been right about the procedure followed to collect the ransom. Josh had to move from public phone to public phone and enter several shopping centers. Eventually, the phone didn't ring and after half an hour of waiting he went back to his car. The trunk had been broken into and the bag had disappeared. Josh hoped that Molino's net had been successful in following whoever had picked up the fake loot.

❧   ❧   ❧

Apparently, the criminals had played a clever game. They had entered the highway from a short unguarded service road closed to the public. The entrance did not appear in the maps available to the police. The service road allowed their quarry to bypass the block that the police had hastily set up on the highway. Molino was impassive but Josh felt that a storm was churning under her external calm.

At the postmortem of the operation held in Molino's office with Molino and Sargent Ellmart, Josh and Amanda present, Amanda insisted a doctor examine Josh. He was all she cared about. His protestations that he felt alright did little to appease her. A police physician was summoned then and there, and Amanda wouldn't leave the room during the examination. The doctor found nothing terribly wrong although the discomfort from the black and blue marks was obvious even to the naked eye.

Shortly after that Molino was ready to continue their discussion. "Yes, a good thing our boy was wearing the body armor and it's too bad we were left with no clues at this point. But we can still try to trace the counterfeit currency as it appears. This may not save the poor kidnap victim but it might lead to an arrest or arrests."

What Josh had seen during the shooting didn't have any substance as if his memory needed time to mature. But as he was sitting there with his thoughts with no particular objective meandering through his mind, the details appeared starkly in his memory. He spoke out.

"It's not true that we are left with nothing. I saw something that may be meaningful. The man who shot me had on Marimondo shoes. They may not be difficult to trace. They cost upward of five hundred dollars. Aside from advertisements, I've only seen them in Mr. Insell's feet."

"My God. Are your sure?" Josh had never seen Molino show excitement before. "If they are unusual we might be able to trace them."

"Oh, shit!" Amanda responded. "They could have been bought any place. They are exported all over the world. Insell travels extensively in foreign countries as well. Doesn't it make more sense to assume they are Insell's and take it from there? I imagine the first thing to do is to check whether Insell has a criminal record."

The hitherto silent Ellmart detached himself from the wall and finally spoke out. "No criminal record. But there are other avenues to follow."

Molino laughed, "Well? Don't keep us in suspense. Did you follow them?" From her expression Josh concluded that she already knew the answer.

Ellmart chuckled. "Of course. There is an interesting account in the press. Arizona, I believe. Somebody named Oswald L. Insell was convicted of swindling an electronics company out of several million dollars about ten years ago. He served three years but the conviction was overturned on appeal. It was found that the prosecutor never informed the defense of several pertinent facts. Apparently the company was all bent from top to bottom. I didn't find any follow up. Perhaps we are dealing with the same man and the L. stands for Louis. Until now this account didn't seem pertinent."

Molino's face became inscrutable again. "Well, we'll have to see whether that information means anything and we'll proceed from there."

The words seemed to be a dismissal. Amanda got up glaring at her and pulling Josh with her. "Don't try to be more informative. You might actually say something!" Then the two of them were gone.

Amanda came frequently to Josh's apartment, even after the black-and-blue marks had faded. She wanted to make sure that he took care of himself. It was a welcome change from the visits of his mother who had not been informed of the latest incident and assumed that he had recovered. He thought he and Amanda might as well live together but he didn't dare voice his conclusion lest it offend her. He still didn't know exactly where he stood with her.

They wondered what was happening with the investigation but they'd heard nothing from the police. After about two weeks a call from Molino finally broke the silence.

"You might want to hear what's new." Her voice had a satisfied ring to it and it arose Josh's curiosity.

"What is it about? What happened?"

"If I wanted to tell you on the phone, I would have said it already. Just come down. You might as well bring your girlfriend."

At the police station they were guided through the stark hallways buzzing with activity to Molino's office. The room was rather bare. Illuminated by fluorescent lights it was bright. There was a photograph of a young boy, of perhaps three or four, on Molino's desk. Sergeant Ellmart came in shortly after their arrival. Molino sitting behind the desk put down the papers she was working on and sat next to the two visitors and the sergeant.

"Hm!" she said.

Josh became impatient. "Is that what you have to tell us?"

"All in due time. I'm pleased to say that our problems have been solved. It's hard to explain without summarizing what we did and what happened. Much of the distinction belongs to Sergeant Ellmart who did a fantastic job. We followed the clue of the shoes and assumed that indeed it was Insell who'd shot Josh. He had been told about the counterfeit money and knew the place where Josh would have his first contact. After all, there had been no reason to suspect the husband and we informed him of what we were doing. Why would Insell kill Josh? The only possible sane motivation would be that he didn't want the ransom to reach the kidnappers, as phony as it was. What could possibly the reason? He might have reason to believe that the absence of the ransom would be a perfect way of disposing the unfortunate Ms. Insell, a crime untraceable to him. In fact, we found out later that one of the kidnappers had the reputation of having killed before.

Then we assumed that Mr. Insell's contact with the criminal world could only have been when he had been incarcerated. Ellmart examined carefully every person he was in contact with in jail and screened them for the crime they had committed. Admittedly he had some luck. One of the names he ran across was Arnold Zwereck. Zwereck has almost never been caught for offenses in his criminal profession. He was in jail for a minor unrelated crime. I don't even remember what it was. But rumors suggested what he specialized in screening and scouting easy targets for other criminals for a fee. In other words he was what we might call a scout or facilitator. As you see it is difficult to find evidence for such an indirect crime. The Sergeant talked to many of the police who had been on the case and worked out what Zwereck actually did in the criminal world."

Josh cleared his throat. Molino raised her head and intoned, "Please don't interrupt. You can ask questions later. At that time, there were serious charges on Zwereck's head since they had finally been able to pin down some of his actions. We offered him a deal with the cooperation of the DA of Madison County where he had been arraigned. Although the crime we were investigating was outside of his jurisdiction, no DA feels comfortable about a major crime going unpunished. Zwereck did indeed inform the kidnappers of a suitable victim. He was following instructions from a unidentified client who paid him cash. Fortunately Zwereck's phones were being tapped under a warrant. To make a long story short, the incautious message of an unidentified stranger was recorded. Insell got careless. Perhaps he didn't think that a call placed from a hotel could be traced to him. The records show that the call was made from the hotel and room where Insell was staying at the time. A similar path through Zwereck's wiretapping was followed to figure out who the kidnappers were. There was nothing that could be used as evidence. However, the blood on the mask which we found in the parking lot after the kidnapping allowed us a DNA match. We found Ms. Insell on a farm one of the kidnappers owned. End of story."

Josh wasn't satisfied. "Do you mean to say that she survived?"

"She's not in great shape, but yes she's okay."

"Thank God. I would feel terrible if she wasn't."

"Well, thank you for your cooperation and I'm glad it ended so well."

But for Josh this wasn't the end of it. Amanda was silent until they reached his apartment.

"Okay. Have you decided is it me or the old strumpet?"

"Do you mean that you've accepted my role in this mess as not indicating a dedication to Maura?"

"Don't play games with me."

"I never was interested in Maura. It was my immaturity taking over. I think I have grown up some. I just couldn't walk away from her with her life in danger. I want you with all my heart. Are you saying that you are accepting me?"

There was a long silence. Then with tears in her eyes Amanda was in his arms.

ABOUT THE AUTHOR

Henry Tedeschi has a background in science. He has taught at the University of Chicago, University of Illinois Medical Center (Chicago) and the State University of New York at Albany. He has written numerous technical articles, several book chapters, a monograph and a textbook in Cell Biology—two printed editions (Academic Press and W.C. Brown) and one edition on the Web. Born in

Italy he was sent to boarding school in Switzerland when Mussolini's racial laws prevented him from attending school in Italy. He spent several formative years in Argentina. He left at age 17 when he immigrated to the U.S. to attend college. He has written fiction and poetry all his life for his own pleasure. He enjoys writing, particularly short stories. He finds writing fiction opens a window into observed details of human behavior, times and places that are otherwise ignored. He has written two mysteries ("*One Day at a Time*" and "*Double*") and four collections of short stories ("*Long and Short Stories*", "*More Long and Short Stories*", "*Three for the Road*" and "*Small Steps*"). The collection in "*Long and Short Stories*" ranges from suspense and mystery to whimsical. They portray a triumph of human values over vicissitudes imposed by situations over which the protagonists have no control. The second collection, More Long and Short Stories, emphasizes the drama and sometimes the comedy of the human condition. Each has a different focus, from the difficulties inherent in encounters between men and women, growing up and aging to the problems of academic life and its frequently unrecognized traumas. "*Three for the Road*" contains longer offerings—two are based in New York, one in the 1820s and another in the 1870s. A third is contemporary and takes place in a South American country under the rule of a cruel dictatorship. All three are stories of suspense and adventure. Most recently, he has published "*Small Steps*", a collection of twenty-five short stories, each representing an important event in somebody's life. Many are about experiences which define a person's future, as well as the hidden aspects of love.

978-0-595-44573-8
0-595-44573-X

Printed in the United States
78501LV00005B/94-117

9 780595 445738